A PISTOL FOR YOUR THOUGHTS . . .

Clint took his gun out and pressed it to the man's nostril.

"What's your name? Why were you following me and the lady all day?"

"F-f-following?"

"Don't try my patience," Clint said, pressing the gun harder into his face.

"Look out!" Sara shouted.

Clint turned in time to see the other man standing over him. He'd left him unconscious at the other end of the alley, his gun thrown into the darkness, but somehow the man had found it.

He should have killed him!

The Gunsmith by J.R. Roberts

MACKLIN'S WOMEN
THE CHINESE GUNMAN
BULLETS AND BALLOTS
THE RIVERBOAT GANG
KILLER GRIZZLY
NORTH OF THE BORDER
EAGLE'S GAP
CHINATOWN HELL
THE PANHANDLE SEARCH
WILDCAT ROUNDUP
THE PONDEROSA WAR
TROUBLE RIDES A FAST HORSE
DYNAMITE JUSTICE
THE POSSE
NIGHT OF THE GILA
THE BOUNTY WOMEN
WILD BILL'S GHOST
THE MINER'S SHOWDOWN
ARCHER'S REVENGE
SHOWDOWN IN RATON
WHEN LEGENDS MEET
DESERT HELL
THE DIAMOND GUN
DENVER DUO
HELL ON WHEELS
THE LEGEND MAKER
WALKING DEAD MAN
CROSSFIRE MOUNTAIN
THE DEADLY HEALER
THE TRAIL DRIVE WAR
GERONIMO'S TRAIL
THE COMSTOCK GOLD FRAUD
TEXAS TRACKDOWN
THE FAST DRAW LEAGUE
SHOWDOWN IN RIO MALO
OUTLAW TRAIL
HOMESTEADER GUNS
FIVE CARD DEATH
TRAILDRIVE TO MONTANA
TRIAL BY FIRE
THE OLD WHISTLER GANG
THE NEVADA TIMBER WAR
NEW MEXICO SHOWDOWN
BARBED WIRE AND BULLETS
DEATH EXPRESS
WHEN LEGENDS DIE
SIX-GUN JUSTICE

MUSTANG HUNTERS
TEXAS RANSOM
VENGEANCE TOWN
WINNER TAKE ALL
MESSAGE FROM A DEAD MAN
RIDE FOR VENGEANCE
THE TAKERSVILLE SHOOT
BLOOD ON THE LAND
SIX-GUN SIDESHOW
MISSISSIPPI MASSACRE
THE ARIZONA TRIANGLE
BROTHERS OF THE GUN
THE STAGECOACH THIEVES
JUDGMENT AT FIRECREEK
DEAD MAN'S JURY
HANDS OF THE STRANGLER
NEVADA DEATH TRAP
WAGON TRAIN TO HELL
RIDE FOR REVENGE
DEAD RINGER
TRAIL OF THE ASSASSIN
SHOOT-OUT AT CROSSFORK
BUCKSKIN'S TRAIL
HELLDORADO
THE HANGING JUDGE
THE BOUNTY HUNTER
TOMBSTONE AT LITTLE HORN
KILLER'S RACE
WYOMING RANGE WAR
GRAND CANYON GOLD
GUNS DON'T ARGUE
GUNDOWN
FRONTIER JUSTICE
GAME OF DEATH
THE OREGON STRANGLER
BLOOD BROTHERS
SCARLET FURY
ARIZONA AMBUSH
THE VENGEANCE TRAIL
THE DEADLY DERRINGER
THE STAGECOACH KILLERS
FIVE AGAINST DEATH
MUSTANG MAN
THE GODFATHER
KILLER'S GOLD
GHOST TOWN

THE GUNSMITH

#128

THE CALIENTE GOLD ROBBERY

SPEAKING VOLUMES, LLC
NAPLES, FLORIDA
2016

THE GUNSMITH
#128 THE CALIENTE GOLD ROBBERY

ISBN 978-1-61232-731-0

THE GUNSMITH

#128

THE CALIENTE GOLD ROBBERY

J.R. ROBERTS

Chapter One

When one entered the hotel called The Silver Spur it was easy to be impressed. It was not as large as some of the other hotels in Portsmouth Square, but it was ostentatiously furnished nonetheless in leather and crystal.

S. D. Jones walked across the lobby to the front desk and waited for the desk clerk to notice that someone was waiting there for assistance. The clerk was a young man in his early twenties, impeccably dressed and groomed. He was busy with something out of sight, and S. D. Jones—being somewhat timid—waited patiently.

Finally, the desk clerk looked up from his work and said, "Can I help you? Would you like a room?"

"A room? No, I'm not here for a room."

"Some gambling, then?"

"No, no gambling."

The clerk, whose name was Tom Royce, frowned at the diminutive person and said, "Then suppose you tell me what you did come here for."

"I'm looking for a man," S. D. Jones said. "I'm told he is staying here."

"We have a few people who live here permanently," Royce said. "What's the man's name?"

"His name," Jones said, "is Adams, Clint Adams."

1

"Oh, I see," Royce said nervously.

"Is he staying here?"

"Uh, yes, he is."

"Would he be in his room now?"

Royce checked his watch and said, "Not right now."

"Well . . . where would he be right now?"

"Having lunch, I suppose," Royce said. "I mean, he's usually having lunch at this time of day."

"Where?"

"In the hotel dining room," Royce said. He inclined his head to his right and said, "Right through that door."

"Thank you," Jones said, and started walking that way.

"Hey, wait!" Royce called.

"Yes?"

"You can't just go in there."

"Why not?" Jones asked. "It's a public dining room, isn't it?"

"He—Mr. Adams, that is—he won't like it if you interrupt his lunch."

"Oh, I see," Jones said. Looking around at the several leather furniture pieces that adorned the lobby, Jones said, "May I sit and wait for him?"

"You can, but—"

At that moment a bellhop came to the desk, a boy who looked to be in his late teens.

"Mrs. Skipp is safe and sound in her room, Tom," he said, leaning on the desk. "You got anything else for me?"

"Sam, someone is looking for Mr. Adams."

"Oh, yeah?" Sam Highbinder said, looking S. D. Jones over. "He'd be having lunch now."

"So I've been told. I'll wait—"

"You could wait," Sam said, "or I could go in and tell him you're here."

"Could you do that?" Jones asked. "I'd be greatly appreciative."

"How appreciative?" Sam Highbinder asked.

It took S. D. Jones a moment to realize what Sam was asking for.

"Oh, I see." Jones reached into a pocket and took out a dollar. It disappeared into Sam's hand and then into his pocket.

"Wait there," Sam said, pointing to a leather divan.

Jones nodded, walked to the divan, and sat down.

"How come Adams doesn't mind when you interrupt his lunch?" Royce asked Sam.

"He likes initiative, Tommy," Sam said, "which is something you don't have."

"You little—"

"Also," Sam said, leaning on the desk so close to Royce that the older man pulled away from him, "I ain't afraid of him and you are—aren't you, Tommy?"

Halfheartedly Royce said, "D-don't call me Tommy."

"Sure, Tommy," Sam said, smiling and moving away from the desk. "Sure."

He turned and went into the dining room. Clint Adams was sitting at his usual table, eating lunch. From the looks of it, the meal was almost over, but Sam knew that Adams would have a second pot of coffee and a piece of cake before he was through.

Warily—because he had lied when he'd told Royce he wasn't afraid of Adams—he approached the table.

Clint Adams loved San Francisco. The city had much to offer in the way of entertainment. Good food, better gambling, and beautiful women. Still, he was starting to grow tired of being in one place, even if it *was* San Francisco.

He looked up from his coffee cup because he could feel someone's eyes on him.

"Sam," he said.

Sam Highbinder wet his lips and said, " 'Afternoon, Mr. Adams."

"You're interrupting my lunch," Clint said.

"I know, sir, but—"

"You'd better have a good reason."

"Oh, I do, Mr. Adams," Sam assured him. "Someone's out in the lobby looking for you."

Clint put his fork down and looked directly into Sam Highbinder's eyes. Nervous as he was, the youngster was able to hold his gaze. Clint knew that the boy was afraid of him—as all of the hotel employees were—but he also knew that Sam Highbinder was the only employee who ever dared to interrupt one of his meals. He'd done it several times before, and Clint had allowed him to get away with it. Clint had been staying at the hotel for over a month now. Because a friend of his owned it he was getting preferential treatment, but he was also being treated well because they knew who he was and were afraid. He didn't like it, but there didn't seem to be much he could do about it.

"What does the person want?"

"I . . . don't know."

"You didn't ask?"

"I, uh, didn't figure it was my place."

"But you did figure it was your place to interrupt my meal."

"Well, uh . . ." Sam didn't know what to say to that.

Of all the employees in the hotel, Sam Highbinder was Clint's favorite. The young man was afraid of him, like the others, but he tried not to show it. Clint enjoyed teasing him.

"Sam, how much was the tip?"

"A dollar."

"A whole dollar?" Clint said, raising his eyebrows. "How often do you get more than two bits as a tip?"

"Only when I help some high roller to his room, Mr. Adams."

"Does this look like a high roller?"

"No, sir. Looks more like a bookkeeper."

"But you were tipped a dollar to announce this bookkeeper type."

"Yes, sir."

"Or was the tip your idea?"

Sam looked down at his shoes now and said, "Well, I may have hinted—"

"Hinted," Clint said, and snorted. "Well, all right. Bring the gentleman in, Sam."

"Uh, it's not a gentleman, Mr.—"

Let's not pass any judgments, Sam. Just do it."

"Yes, sir."

"And Sam?"

"Yes, sir?" the bellboy said, half turned in his tracks.

"Don't expect a tip from me," Clint said. "That dollar should cover it admirably."

"Oh, sure, yes, sir."

As Sam Highbinder turned and left the dining room, Clint waved for the waitress to bring the second pot of coffee. She was a small, compactly built girl in her early twenties who had only been working there a week, but already she knew that Clint was a special guest of the hotel, a personal friend of the hotel owner.

He sat back and waited for his second pot of coffee and for the dollar tipper to arrive.

"Mr. Adams," Highbinder said moments later, "this is S. D. Jones."

"All right, Sam. Get lost."

"Yes, sir."

Jones stood there staring at Clint.

"Sit down, please."

Jones started at the sound of Clint's voice and hastily took the seat across from him.

"What can I do for you?"

"I, uh, I want—" Jones began, but stopped when the waitress came with the pot of coffee.

"Thanks, Leona," Clint said.

She smiled and backed away from the table.

"Wait," Clint said to her, and she stopped. He looked at Jones and asked, "Would you like a cup of coffee?"

"Uh, yes, thank you."

Clint said to Leona, "Leona, bring another cup, please."

"Yes, sir, Mr. Adams."

As she went to get the cup, Clint said, "Suppose you start talking, Jones."

"Oh, of course," Jones said. A hand went up to smooth hair that didn't need smoothing. A nervous gesture.

"I've come to hire you, Mr. Adams."

"For what?"

"Well, perhaps I should explain who I am first."

"Let's hear that startling revelation, then."

Chapter Two

"I am a Wells Fargo agent, assigned to Caliente, California."

In spite of himself Clint *did* find that fact startling. It was difficult to imagine this harmless, timid-looking thing as an agent of Wells Fargo.

"In fact, I am the only Wells Fargo agent in Caliente."

"In all of Caliente, eh?" Clint asked, widening his eyes.

"Oh, well, it's not all that big," Jones said.

Leona came with the extra cup, and glared at Jones while pouring the extra cupful.

"Kind of you," Jones said, adding sugar.

Clint winced as the sugar melted into the coffee, turning it into something undrinkable, and said, "Yeah."

If cream gets anywhere near that coffee, he thought, I'll shoot.

Jones poured cream into the coffee, and Clint didn't shoot.

"What does Wells Fargo want with me?" Clint asked. "I'm sure they have countless men of varying degrees of competence— "

"Excuse me for interrupting you," Jones said, "but it isn't Wells Fargo who wants to hire you, Mr. Adams. *I* want to hire you, myself."

"All right," Clint said, "what do *you* want to hire me for?"

"I must explain something."

"Then do it!" Clint said impatiently.

S. D. Jones explained that the Holliday & Bayer Bank of Los Angeles had recently begun to flounder badly, so the sum of $250,000 in gold pieces was being sent from San Francisco to help them ride out their difficulty.

"It's going to take two hundred and fifty thousand dollars to save them, and you call it 'difficulty'?"

"Well, perhaps that is a bit of an understatement. Uh, may I continue?"

"Please do."

Jones told Clint that the money was coming in on the Southern Pacific Railroad but that the railroad was not yet completed and that Caliente was the end of the line.

"Once the money reaches there," she said, "I'm afraid it becomes my responsibility to make sure it reaches Los Angeles by Wells Fargo coach."

"I see. It's quite a responsibility."

"Yes, one I'm not sure I am up to, I don't mind admitting."

"Tell that to your bosses."

"Uh, well, I don't mind admitting it to *you*, that is," Jones said somewhat sheepishly.

"Well then, why don't you admit to me what it is you want me to do?"

Jones sipped some coffee first, then set the cup down very gingerly on the table.

"I'd like you to help me make sure that gold reaches Los Angeles safely."

"Don't tell me," Clint said. "You don't want Wells Fargo to know about me."

"There's no need," Jones said. "I'm hiring you myself. It's a personal matter."

"I'm not sure your employers would look at it that way," Clint said.

"Will you take the job, Mr. Adams?"

The hangdog look on Jones's face was so hopeful that it grated on Clint's teeth. He drank some coffee, but it wasn't hot enough to wash the taste away.

"I really can't see how I could—" he started, but S. D. Jones interrupted him.

"I'll pay you a thousand dollars."

Clint stopped, then said, "I'm sorry, but—"

"Two thousand."

Clint frowned across the table.

"You did say that *you* were hiring me, and not Wells Fargo?"

Jones looked embarrassed and said, "I have some money of my own that I inherited. I don't use it much— I need very little— but I'd like to use it to save my . . . my reputation."

Clint studied Jones's face for a few moments, then called Leona over.

"Yes, Mr. Adams?"

"Bring me a pot of hot coffee, will you?"

"I just brought you—"

"This one isn't hot anymore," he said patiently. "May I have another?"

"Y-yes, sir."

She picked up the pot and hurried away.

"Mr. Adams?"

"I haven't forgotten you."

Jones remained silent, waiting for Clint's reply. Clint really wasn't looking for a job, but if he was going to take one he figured he might as well be well paid for it. Besides, the hopeful look on the Wells Fargo agent's face was hard to take.

"All right," Clint finally said.

"You'll do it?"

"For twenty-five hundred dollars."

"Done!"

"And two conditions."

"What are they?"

"You won't have any coffee from my new pot."

"One cup is enough for me," S. D. Jones said. "What's the other condition?"

"You answer a question."

"What question?"

"What does the S. D. stand for?"

S. D. Jones smiled slightly and said, "Sara Denise."

Chapter Three

"How did Sara Denise Jones become a Wells Fargo agent?" Clint asked.

"You said one question, Mr. Adams," Sara Jones said, rising. "When can we leave for Caliente?"

"When is the train due to arrive?"

"A week from tomorrow."

"We'll leave in the morning, then," he said.

"Wonderful," she said. "I'll see you then. Shall we meet out front?"

"How did you get here?" Clint asked.

"Stagecoach."

"And where are you staying?"

She shrugged and said, "I haven't registered at a hotel yet."

"Then stay here."

"I doubt I can afford it."

"I thought you had money."

"Not to waste on overpriced hotel—"

"Not overpriced," he said. "Free."

"Free?" she asked, frowning. "I don't underst—"

"The owner of this hotel is a friend of mine. Find Sam—the kid who brought you in and bilked you out of a dollar—and tell him I said to get you a room."

"Mr. Adams, you don't have to—"

"We'll be able to get an early start if we both leave from here," he said. "Might even be able to get some breakfast first."

S. D. Jones hesitated, then nodded and said, "Well, all right. Thank you."

"Don't look so nervous," he said. "All the doors in this hotel have locks."

"Oh, I wasn't thinking—"

"That's the case I find with a lot of women," he said. "Go and find Sam."

She didn't like what he'd said about women, but he intimidated her, so she didn't say anything. He was hoping she would have. It would have shown that she had spunk.

"All right," she said.

She turned and left the dining room. If Clint was any judge, she was about thirty. She acted younger, but she had a job only an adult should have. Being a Wells Fargo agent was no easy thing, even in Caliente. She must have had some ability to get the job. Either that or she was somebody's daughter—or mistress.

The waitress, Leona, came back carrying a fresh pot of coffee.

Clint went to Terence White's office and found his friend there.

"Terry, I'm putting a woman up for the night."

"What you do with your room is your business," Terry White said. He was a tall, slender man in his early forties. He wore a carefully groomed goatee, and his hair came to a widow's peak. It combined to give him what he called a "Mephistophelian" look.

Clint just said he looked like the devil himself.

"Very funny."

"Who is she?"

"A Wells Fargo agent."

"Now I know you're kidding."

"No, I'm not."

"What the hell—"

"I'll be leaving with her in the morning, so I want her to spend the night here."

"A job?"

"Yes."

"Doing what?"

Clint paused, then said, "Riding shotgun."

"I didn't know you were looking for that kind of work," his friend said.

"I wasn't."

"Playing poker tonight?"

White played in a regular game in which Clint had been playing since his arrival.

"I'm not sure," Clint said.

"See you there if you do."

"Yeah."

Clint turned and went to the door. With his hand on the doorknob he turned and said, "That new girl in the dining room? Leona something?"

"Gore," White said. "What about her?"

Clint hesitated a moment, then shook his head and said, "Nothing."

After Clint had removed his boots and shirt, there was a knock on the door. He frowned, remembering what he had told Sara Jones about the locks on the door. Could she be checking to see if he was right? No, she didn't seem to be the type to visit a man in his hotel room.

He walked to the door, opened it, and was surprised to see Leona Gore standing in the hall.

"Leona."

"Surprised?" she asked.

"Yes."

"So am I," she said. "May I come in?"

"Sure . . ." he said, backing away from the door. He was more than a little bit puzzled as she walked past him. She had obviously come up straight from work, because she hadn't changed her clothes. He could smell the tartness of her perspiration and did not find it unpleasant.

When he closed the door and turned to face her she said, "I guess you're wondering why I'm here."

"I am a little curious."

"We've been giving each other looks ever since I started working here, Clint, and even though you scare me a little, I thought it was time we did something about it."

"You're afraid of me?"

"You know I am," she said. "Everyone in the hotel who knows who you are is afraid of you. Isn't that the way you want it?"

"No, it's not," he said. "I don't want anyone to be afraid of me."

"But . . . you enjoy it. Look at the way you tease poor Sam Highbinder."

"Sometimes I find it funny," he said, "and sometimes it's annoying, but there's not much I can do about it."

"Well . . ." she said, hesitating, "what about us? Is there something we can do about that?"

He hesitated this time and then said, "Yes, I'm sure there is."

He walked to her, took her by the shoulders, and kissed her. Her tongue slid eagerly into his mouth as she melted against him. He reached for the hem of her workdress and lifted it, running his hands over her thighs. When he lifted the dress higher she raised her arms so he could pull it over her head. He was pleasantly shocked to find that she was wearing no underclothes.

She saw the look on his face and said, "Underthings bother me while I'm working. I hope you don't mind."

"I don't mind at all," he said.

He ran his hands down her back and over her buttocks, then cupped them and pulled her to him for another kiss. Her breasts were full and firm against his chest, the nipples very hard. He backed her up until her thighs were against the bed, and then pushed her so she fell on it. He removed the rest of his clothes and then crawled on top of her. She wrapped her arms around him and lifted and spread her legs. He found her wet and ready, and slid right into her. She moaned and pulled his head down so he could lick her breasts, tasting the salt of her perspiration while he moved in and out of her. As they both neared the peak of their passion she lifted his head for a kiss that muffled both of their cries. . . .

Chapter Four

When they reached Caliente Sara Jones took Clint to her office. It was a small, one-room affair just off the main street with barely enough room for a desk, a file cabinet, and a safe. On one wall was a map of the area. On another was a map of California.

"This is it, huh?"

"This is it," she said, nodding her head. "Not much, huh?"

"When will the stage arrive?"

"Day after tomorrow. The train gets in at seven A.M."

"Who'll meet it?"

"I will, along with Jerome Stockton, the chief of police of Caliente."

"I'll want to meet Stockton."

"I'll arrange it for tomorrow."

"Fine," he said. "I'll check into a hotel and meet you here in the morning."

"What about dinner?"

"I'll get it in the hotel dining room."

"No, I meant—never mind," she stammered. "I'll meet you here tomorrow morning."

He studied her for a moment. All during their trip to Caliente they'd spoken very little. That was by Clint's choice. All he had to know about her was that she was hiring him to do a job. To do it, he didn't need to get to know her better, or to know her background.

He still gauged her to be about thirty. If he looked at her critically he'd say she needed a new hairdo and some makeup and then she might even be attractive. She was tall and slender, almost willowy, with well-formed breasts and hips. If she dressed differently in something other than a severely cut suit . . .

That was enough critical study.

"I need a small hotel," he said.

"There's a fine one just down the street—"

"A small one," he said.

"Well . . . there's a small one at the south end of town, but that's not the best section—"

"That'll be fine," he said. He walked to the door, then turned and said, "In the morning," and left.

Caliente was a decent-size town in the Tehachapi Mountains, southeast of Bakersfield. It had a nine-man police force headed by Chief of Police Jerome Stockton, a big, florid-faced man with white muttonchops who had political ambitions. Stockton knew, however, that before his ambitions could go any farther he was going to have to get out of these goddamned mountains.

Stockton was seated behind his desk, trying to figure out a way to do this, when there was a knock on his door.

"Come in."

The door opened and Officer Carl Pressman entered.

"Sir, Miss Jones from Wells Fargo is out here to see you."

Stockton knew Sara Jones. They didn't know each other well, but that didn't prevent them from being polite to each other when they passed in the street or met in a restaurant.

Stockton had been a policeman in Caliente for nine years and chief of police for four of them. Sara Jones had been the local Wells Fargo agent for only eighteen months. During that time they had not had the opportunity—or the reason—to visit each other's office.

"Miss Jones?" Stockton said with interest. "Well, show her in, officer."

"Yes, sir."

Stockton opened his top drawer and took out a hand mirror. He checked his mustache and muttonchops and gave himself a quick critical appraisal. At fifty-one he was carrying more weight than he had ever carried in his life, but he felt that the extra bulk gave him more of a physical presence. His face had filled out, but it was still smooth-skinned and not unattractive. He was generally considered to be one of Caliente's more eligible bachelors.

He put the hand mirror away hastily as the door opened. Officer Pressman stepped in, and then stepped aside to allow S. D. Jones to enter. He'd chew Pressman's head off later for not knocking before entering. He'd almost been caught with his vanity hanging out.

"Miss Jones," he said, rising and moving around his desk. "How nice to see you."

"Chief Stockton," Sara Jones said.

To Stockton, Sara Jones was especially pleasing to the eye. She was attractive but not flashy. She'd make a fine politician's wife. He did not agree with Wells Fargo's decision to assign a woman to the post she held, but he'd often thought about inviting her to dinner to supply the opportunity to get to know her better.

Maybe now was the time.

"Please, sit down," Stockton said, shaking her hand. She had a firm grip. To Stockton that was also in her favor. "May I offer you a drink?"

"No, thank you, Chief," she said, seating herself. "I came here for a specific reason."

"Well, to business then," he said, seating himself behind his desk. When they got that out of the way maybe he'd invite her to dinner. "What can I do for you?"

Up to now Sara Jones had told Stockton nothing of the gold that was coming into Caliente day after tomorrow. Now she told him the whole story, starting with the difficulties being suffered by the Holliday & Bayer Bank of Los Angeles, to the arrival of $250,000 in gold in Caliente by train By the time she finished her story, Chief Jerome Stockton had ceased to think of her as a possible dinner partner or future first lady.

He was seething with anger.

"Why wasn't I told of this earlier?" he demanded.

"There was no reason for you—"

"No reason!" he shouted, cutting her off. "My dear young lady, I am the chief of police in this town. I have every reason to know what's going on. You had no right to make such arrangements without contacting me first."

"I beg your pardon, Chief, but Wells Fargo had no such obligation. In fact, I'm only notifying you now out of common courtesy. I felt you should be made aware of the fact that a sum of gold of this magnitude would be entering your jurisdiction."

Stockton opened his mouth to reply, then closed it quickly. He waited a moment while he regained control of his temper.

"Miss Jones, you understand that I will wish to be present at the train station when this gold arrives."

"Of course," she said. "But you will understand the need for secrecy in this matter, Chief."

Stockton bristled.

"I am not in the habit of passing on idle gossip, madam."

"No, of course you're not," she said, rising before the chief lost control of his temper again. "I propose we discuss this again tomorrow. I have engaged an extra man to help with the security."

"I have sufficient men to deal with that problem," Stockton said. The chief was getting very stiff-necked.

"I'm sure you have, Chief," Sara Jones said. "Nevertheless, I have engaged him."

"Well, I'll want to meet him and check him out."

That was exactly what she had hoped he would say. If *she* had suggested that Clint meet Stockton, the chief might have wanted to know why. It was much better that the meeting be his idea.

"I'll bring him around in the afternoon," she said, "and we can coordinate security."

"I really wish you'd given me more time, Miss Jones," he complained.

"I have every confidence in you, Chief," she said. "I'll see you tomorrow."

Stockton remained seated while S. D. Jones left his office. Annoyed with the woman, he took out his hand mirror and examined his face, stroking his mustache with his finger.

Calmer now, he put the mirror away, stood and shouted at the top of his lungs, "Pressman!"

Sara Denise Jones stood just outside the police station and took a deep breath. She had disliked Chief Stockton since the first moment they'd met, and this meeting had only intensified the feeling. For the past eighteen months she'd been afraid that he was going to ask her to have dinner with him, or go for a buggy ride—or worse.

After the tone of this meeting maybe she didn't have to worry about that anymore.

Wanting dinner, she found herself walking toward Clint's hotel, and stopped herself short. He was an odd man. Violent, to be sure—both his reputation and his demeanor suggested that— but also attractive . . . and repellent.

She'd never met a man like him before.

She reversed direction and went to a small café for dinner, where she ate alone—as she had done every night for the past eighteen months.

Chapter Five

Clint found his hotel satisfactory.

It was small and a little seedy. When he was in San Francisco he stayed in the best hotels and ate at the best restaurants. When he was working he stayed in the most out-of-the-way hotels and ate in small cafés.

He checked in and asked the bored-looking clerk, "Do you have bathing facilities?"

"We sure do," the clerk said. He looked up from the desk and when he saw Clint he froze. He'd never seen the man before, but he knew what he was looking at. "Oh, s-sure, yes, sir, we do."

"Have a warm bath drawn for me. I'll be back down in ten minutes."

"Yes, sir," the clerk said, eager to please. "It'll be ready, sir." As Clint walked to the stairs, the young man called out nervously, "I'll draw it myself."

Clint ignored the man, tucked his bedroll under his arm, and went up to his room. He traveled light and dressed not nearly as well as he did when he was in San Francisco.

The room was about what he expected: a bed with a paper-thin mattress, a small dresser with a pitcher and bowl on top of it, and one rickety-looking straight-backed wooden chair.

He left his gear in the room and went back downstairs for his bath.

The man standing across the street from the hotel had followed Clint there. He'd spotted him coming out of the Wells Fargo office, and that was only because he had been watching the Wells Fargo office. He'd recognized him immediately and followed him to the hotel. Now that the big man was in the hotel, the tail left his vantage point and went to find the others.

Everybody had to know that Clint was in town—and it couldn't be a coincidence.

He was in the tub soaking before he realized that there were no towels in the one tubroom.

"Shit," he said.

His enjoyment of the bath ruined, he stood up and stepped out and, naked, left the room to pad down the hall to tear the clerk a new asshole. As he approached the curtained doorway that led to the lobby, he heard voices.

"Please," a woman said, "I just came here for a room."

"Well, honey, you're in luck," a man said, "because we got two of 'em."

"Please . . . don't touch me!"

Clint sighed, walked back to the bathroom, retrieved his gun, and went back down the hall. There were the sounds of a struggle on the other side of the curtain as he walked through and stepped into the lobby.

Three men had a woman pinned to the wall along the stairway. One of the men had his hands on her, while the other two were hemming her in so she couldn't get away from them. Clint didn't have much time to examine her, but she seemed both fairly young and attractive.

And, at the moment, at a clear disadvantage.

On the floor in the center of the lobby was the desk clerk, bleeding from the head where he had obviously been pistol-whipped.

"Come on, sweetheart," one of the men was saying, "the clerk can't give you a room until he wakes up. We'll give you one of ours—with us in it."

Clint walked around behind the desk and brought his hand down on the bell. All eyes suddenly turned to him the three men curious and then angry, the girl pleading.

Clint held up a key and said, "I have a room for the woman."

"Who the hell are you?" one of the men asked.

"I'm the new desk clerk." Clint was still wet, and he was cold. He'd been mildly annoyed about not having a towel. Now he was becoming very annoyed.

"You'd better mind your own business, fella," a second man said.

The third man was considerably larger than the other two and had nothing to say. He was obviously the muscle.

"I am," Clint said. "I need a towel, and I don't know where they're kept. If you hadn't put him to sleep," he added, inclining his head toward the sleeping clerk, "he'd be able to tell me. *You're* interfering with *me*."

"I'll interfere with you," one of them said. He was the one who had been pawing the woman. In fact, he still had one hand on her arm.

"Be my guest," Clint said.

"Moose, interfere with the man," the man said to the biggest of the three.

As the big man started to approach, Clint noticed that he did not wear a gun. Also, from the man's bulk, Clint wasn't quite sure he'd be able to take him hand to hand—especially not if the other two joined the fray.

Well, Clint had no intention of trying them—not naked, anyway—and he had no intention of taking a beating, especially not for a woman he didn't know.

Clint's other hand—the one holding his gun—had been below the level of the desk, and now he brought it up. Moose stopped.

"Keep going, Moose," the spokesman said. "He won't shoot an unarmed man."

Clint looked at the man with raised eyebrows.

"Do you know me?" he asked.

"Never saw you before."

"Then what makes you think I won't shoot?"

The man looked smug.

"Because your kind never do."

"And what kind is that?"

"The do-gooder kind," the man said. "The kind who rushes to help a woman he don't even know."

"Hey, fella," Clint said, "I'm standing here freezing my butt off—my naked butt—because I don't have a towel. If you hadn't knocked him out," he said, pointing to the man on the floor, "I wouldn't be freezing. That's my beef with you."

The smug look stayed in place.

"Keep going, Moose," he said. "Turn this fella into *chipped* beef."

Moose started forward again.

Clint fired one shot into the man's left kneecap. Moose's mouth opened and a shrill scream escaped as he grabbed his knee and went down. It took a moment for Clint to realize that the woman had screamed as well.

Both of the other men instinctively moved for their guns, but Clint pointed his at them and said, "Hold it, boys!"

"You're in a lot of trouble now, friend," the spokesman said.

"Go and tell it to the law."

"Don't think we won't."

"Pick up your friend and get out. I kind of liked shooting off his kneecap. It could get to be a nasty habit."

Both men moved forward and picked Moose up and dragged him, still screaming, out of the lobby.

The woman stayed where she was against the wall, still looking terrified—only this time it was Clint who terrified her.

"You shot that man," she said, her tone accusatory.

"I was here, too, lady," he reminded her. "I know what I did."

"But . . . he wasn't armed."

"You don't think so, huh?"

He came around the desk, unmindful of his nudity, and leaned over the desk clerk. The man was breathing regularly, which indicated he wasn't hurt badly.

"Come on," Clint said, slapping the man's face, "I need a towel."

Chapter Six

Officer Pressman showed Clint into Chief Stockton's office.

"Your name Clint?"

"You know that already," Clint said. "You sent your man to the hotel to get me, so you know who I am."

"You got a smart mouth."

"Only people who aren't as smart as me think so."

Stockton sat behind his desk and fumed.

"Sit," he said.

Pressman put his hand out to push Clint, but Clint had already moved. He sat down opposite the chief and folded his hands in his lap.

"Get out, Pressman," Stockton said.

"Yes, sir."

After Pressman left, Stockton stood up. Clint watched him. The police chief stood and stretched to his full height of six feet and paused a moment. Clint wondered why, since there was no woman in the room for him to pose for.

"You're an impressive figure of a man, Chief, no doubt about it," Clint said.

Stockton's back stiffened and he glared at Clint.

"I have a complaint against you, Adams, that you shot an unarmed man."

"Did you see the man, Chief?"

"I did."

"A man that size look unarmed to you?"

"Admittedly he was a formidable man, but the fact is he was not armed."

"He was going to pound me into the floor," Clint said.

"Mr. Adams, you look like a man who can handle yourself."

"I can . . . but not against three men, two of whom *were* armed."

"They weren't involved—"

"That's what they say. Did you talk to the woman?"

"Julie Collins," the chief said. "I spoke to her."

"What did she say?"

"That you were naked," Stockton said, disapproval plain in his tone.

"What else did she say, Chief?"

"That you helped her."

"And I did."

"You could have helped her without shooting anyone."

"Look, Chief, you had to be there," Clint said. "I *was* naked, which makes a man feel a little vulnerable. There were three of them, two with guns backing up the one who didn't have a gun. You think that if I had engaged this one in hand-to-hand combat his friends would have stayed out of it?"

"All I know is—"

"Do those three live in town?"

"No, they're passing through."

"As am I. You don't know them any better than you know me. Why would you take their word against mine?"

"Because I know your type, Adams."

"What type is that?"

"You're a killer," Stockton said. "I've dealt with your kind before. You like killing."

"I kneecapped him, didn't I?" Clint said. "I didn't kill him. You think I missed at that range and meant to kill him?"

"You crippled that man for life."

"He would have crippled me if I hadn't."

"That's debatable."

"The whole matter is debatable."

Stockton wanted to make it hard on Clint, but both statements were true.

"In light of what you did for that young woman," Stockton said, "I'm inclined to dismiss the man's complaint against you."

"You're a real gentleman, Chief."

Stockton gave Clint a quick look to see if he was being sarcastic.

"What if I wanted to make a complaint against them?" Clint asked.

"I'd say don't push your luck, Mr. Adams."

"Can I go?"

"You can go," Stockton said, "but I'd suggest you leave town, Mr. Adams. I do not want to see you again in Caliente. Understand?"

"Oh, I understand, Chief," Clint said, standing up.

"You don't have any remorse, do you?" Stockton asked, as Clint started for the door.

"About what?"

"About crippling that poor man."

"Chief, I wonder how many men that 'poor man' has crippled in the past. That was what he did, you know. He crippled people, whenever the other man told him to. Well, not this time—and maybe never again. Besides—"

"Besides . . . what?"

"I needed a goddamn towel!"

Chapter Seven

Sara Denise Jones was just finishing her dinner when Clint walked into the café. She was surprised. He had indicated to her that he would be eating dinner at his hotel.

Their eyes met as soon as he entered, and she stood up and waved him over.

"Miss Jones," he said when he reached her table.

"Mr. Adams," she said. "I would have thought you'd had dinner by now."

"I've had sort of an eventful evening," Clint said, "and it hasn't included dinner."

"Then please join me."

He looked as if he wanted to refuse, but after she sat, so did he.

"Thank you," he said.

"Their stew is quite good."

When the waiter came over Clint said, "I'll have the stew, and a beer."

"Bread?" the man asked.

"Yes."

"Miss Jones—"

"Please, Mr. Adams, call me Sara."

"Sara," he said. "You can call me . . . Clint."

30

"Tell me about your evening."

"I went looking for a towel," he said, "and found trouble."

He gave her a brief explanation of the incident, ending with his meeting with Stockton.

"That will make tomorrow rather awkward," she said. "That's when I was intending to introduce you. What do we do now?"

"Just introduce me, and let me handle it," Clint said. "It was a good idea to tell him that I was extra security. He'll think I was hired by Wells Fargo."

"That was my point."

The waiter came with Clint's dinner, and Sara asked for coffee.

After the waiter left she said, "It was kind of you."

"What was?"

"Helping that woman."

The whole incident still annoyed him, and he reacted to her remark badly.

"Don't try to make me out something I'm not, Sara."

"You didn't help her?"

"I did," Clint said, "but it was incidental."

"To looking for a towel."

"Yes."

"I see."

He tasted his stew and found that she was right. It was very good.

"The chief strikes me as something of a peacock," he said.

"He is. He's considered quite a catch by most of the women in town," Sara said. "Matrons, mostly."

"And you?"

"I can't stand him."

"Why not?"

"Because he believes it, too."

"Has he tried—"

"Not yet," she said. "I had been expecting it, but after my meeting with him today I doubt that it will happen."

"Why?"

"He was quite upset with me for not informing him of the gold shipment sooner."

"And me?"

"And about you," she said. "He took it as an insult against his men."

"Well, let him huff and puff all he wants," Clint said. "The point is to keep that gold of yours safe, and that's what we'll do."

"Good."

She had a second cup of coffee, but Clint was eating so slowly that her presence at the table was starting to become awkward.

"Well, I hope you won't mind if I move on," she said finally.

"No, not at all," Clint said.

Sara had the feeling that he preferred eating alone. In fact, he seemed a man who would prefer his own company to that of others most of the time.

She wondered idly about him and . . . and women.

"I'll see you in the morning, then," she said, standing up.

"I'll take care of your bill."

"You don't have to do that."

"Why not?" he asked. "It's your money I'll be using."

"You have a point there," she said. "All right. See you tomorrow."

"Right."

She couldn't resist.

"Try to stay out of trouble, will you?"

"I always do," he said without looking up.

•   •   •

Two men stood across the street from the café and watched Sara Jones leave.

"He's still in there," one of them said.

"Obviously."

"You think he's here about the gold?"

"How do I know?" the first man said. "He's with the girl, isn't he? That's got to mean something."

"Maybe he's sweet on her."

"Does he look like the kind of man who would be sweet on that kind of woman?"

"What's the matter with her? She's nice-looking enough."

"A little too plain, for my taste."

"Do you think Teddy is right about him?"

"If Teddy says he's trouble, then he's trouble," the other man said.

"Well," the first man said, "he won't be anymore . . . not after tonight."

The second part of his dinner went more quickly. He had deliberately eaten the first part slowly to see how patient she was. Clint tested people he did business with. Sometimes they were trivial tests, like this one, and sometimes more serious.

"Anything else, sir?" the waiter asked.

"Coffee," Clint said. "A pot."

"Yes, sir."

Clint had taken this job because it seemed simple enough. Riding shotgun on a stagecoachload of gold from Caliente to Los Angeles. Easy work, and not time-consuming. He did not intend to let a run-in with the chief of police make the job any harder. Having met Stockton, he decided that a touch of diplomacy might be better used when he met Stockton tomorrow for a second time.

The two men across the street watched Clint leave the café.

"It's about time," the first man said.

"Your problem is you have no patience."

"Let's follow him."

"Think he's headed back to his hotel?"

"This early?" the first man said. "Most likely the saloon."

"And we stick with him?"

"Until the proper circumstance arises."

"Huh?"

"Until we get a clear shot at him," the first man said patiently.

"Why didn't you say so in the first place?"

Clint stepped into the first saloon he came to, confident that the two men following him would stay with him but stay outside. They wouldn't want to risk being spotted—not knowing that they had been spotted a long time ago. Actually, Clint had seen the first man watching him earlier in the day, and had been expecting either the same man or someone else to take up the vigil. Since there were two now, however, it was fairly obvious that they intended to do more than watch.

The place was small and doing a brisk business. There were several women working the room, and most of the tables were taken.

Clint went to the bar and ordered a beer.

He knew he wanted to stay out of trouble tonight, but if he went back outside to go to his hotel he was going to have to deal with those two men. Another run-in with Stockton before tomorrow would not be advisable.

As he was trying to figure out a way of avoiding the two men without engaging them, one of the girls came up to him and said, "Hi, my name's Candy. Want some company?"

He looked down and saw that the girl really was a "girl," eighteen if she was a day—and if her name was "Candy," then his was Moses.

"What are you doing out this late?" he asked. "Does your mother know where you are?"

She made a face at him and said, "Oh, you must like older women. I'll send Darleen over."

"Which one is Darleen?"

"The redhead with the wrinkles," the girl said.

Clint looked across the room and saw Darleen. She did indeed have red hair, a great mass of it, but the wrinkles were in the eyes of the beholder. To the eighteen-year-old standing next to him Darleen—who appeared to be about thirty-two or so—must have seemed old.

To Clint she was just right, and was the answer to his dilemma.

"Why don't you do that, little girl?" he said to Candy. "Send Darleen right over here."

Chapter Eight

Clint woke the next morning with a warm weight resting against his hip. He rolled over to look at Darleen, who was curled up against him like a cat.

Clint had been right about Darleen. She was thirty-two and had been plying her craft for a long time, since she was younger than Candy. It got tiring, she said, but when she was with the right man, it could still be pleasurable.

During the night, each time they had sex, she had acted as if it was *extremely* pleasurable, but she was, after all, a whore. Whores could make a man think he was the best lover in the world just by moaning and groaning a little and wiggling their butt.

Still, Clint had some experience himself, and if he was any judge, the woman he knew as "Darleen" had enjoyed their lovemaking each time. He had taken her swiftly the first time, and brutally, but later had made it gentle for her. The third time it was she who was the aggressor, climbing atop him and doing most of the work.

He slid out of bed easily, so as not to wake her, but she was sleeping so soundly she wouldn't have budged if he had fired a shot.

He moved to the window and looked outside. He'd asked her if she had a room that overlooked the street, and when she brought him to this room the first thing he had done was check the street. By staring long enough his eyes had become accustomed to the night and he'd been able to make out the two men in a doorway across the street. Now he looked at that same doorway and saw one man, seemingly asleep in it. They had probably taken turns during the night keeping watch, waiting for him to come out.

He started to get dressed and was strapping on his gun when she woke up. She smiled up at him sleepily and stretched her lithe body. She was slender, but she had large breasts with big brown nipples. As full as her breasts were, if you looked just a little lower you were able to see the outlines of her ribs.

"I know I'm too skinny," she said, "except for . . . these." She cupped her breasts and held them up to him, wrinkling her nose.

"You're fine," he said.

She sat up, not bothering to cover her breasts.

"Are they still out there?"

"Who?"

"Whoever you were avoiding by staying here with me," she said, pushing a strand of hair behind one ear. "I know you didn't stay with me because of my . . . just because of me."

"They're still out there," he said. "One of them, anyway."

"What do they want?"

"I didn't ask."

"Will you?"

"If the opportunity arises."

"You're not afraid of them," she said. "I know that."

"How do you know that?"

"You don't strike me as a man who is afraid . . . of anything. But what are you afraid of?"

"I don't know," Clint said. "I haven't found it yet . . . but it's there, believe me."

"I believe it if you do."

He moved to the window again and looked out. The doorway was empty now.

"Gone?" she asked.

Her nodded.

"How long will you be in town?"

"Until tomorrow."

"Come back, then," she said. "Tonight . . . if you like."

"I can't say right now."

"That's fine," she said, shrugging her shoulders. She lay down and stretched luxuriously, enjoying the way his eyes raked her body.

"I'm going to get some more sleep. Pull the door shut on your way out?"

"Sure."

She closed her eyes and had drifted off even before he left.

Chapter Nine

Clint went to his hotel for a bath and a change of clothes, and then went to meet Sara Jones out front. She was waiting on the boardwalk when he came out.

"Good morning," she said.

"Good morning."

"Did you sleep well?"

"Well enough."

"Shall we have some breakfast?"

"Why not?"

She frowned studying him and said, "Is anything wrong?"

"I'll tell you at breakfast," he said. "Come on, let's get off the street."

Later, as they were finishing, Sara asked Clint, "Do you know for sure that they want you dead?"

"Maybe they do and maybe they don't," Clint said. "Could be just somebody with an old beef against me that put them on my tail."

"Are there a lot of people like that?"

"Like what?"

"With a beef against you?"

He hesitated before answering.

"Too many to count."

"How about friends?"

He looked at her and said, "I've got my fair share, I guess. Maybe less than most people."

"That bother you?"

"Which one?"

"Either one."

He shook his head.

"No."

"Why not?"

"Because I can't control how people feel about me, Sara, so there's no use crying about it, or worrying about it."

"Sure you could control it . . . if you cared enough to."

He ignored the comment.

"You don't like it when people get personal, do you?" she asked.

"That depends on who the people are," he said. He stared at her until she looked away. "And how about you, Sara?"

"What about me?"

"Do you like it when people get personal?"

"I . . . don't know what you mean," she said, looking at her plate.

"Sure you do, Sara," he said. "You're a little too timid to start conversations like this. You can't follow them up, and you can't handle it when they get turned around."

"I'll remember that," she said, jabbing her fork into her eggs.

"Don't get touchy, now."

"I'm not . . . I'm not touchy," she said morosely. "Why don't we just finish our breakfast and go to see the chief?"

"I thought we were going to see him in the afternoon," he said.

"What would you suggest we do until then?"

"I could think of a few things," he said, staring at her boldly.

She really got flustered this time, blushing, and didn't know where to look or what to do.

"All right," he said. "We'll go to see the chief and talk about security."

"Are you going to tell him about the men following you?"

"I'm not going to tell him any more than I have to," Clint said.

"Why not?"

"Because I don't like him any more than you do."

Chapter Ten

Officer Pressman showed Clint and Sara Jones into Chief Stockton's office. Stockton was hastily putting something into the top drawer of his desk.

"How many times have I told you not to open that door without knocking?" he snapped at the young officer.

"Sorry, Chief."

"Get out!"

"Yes, sir."

Pressman backed out and closed the door.

Stockton looked at Clint as if he'd just recognized him.

"What are you doing here?" he demanded. "I thought I told you to leave town."

"Asked," Clint said. "You suggested that I leave town."

"Told, suggested," Stockton said, shaking his head. "Why are you still here?"

"I'm working."

"Working?" Stockton repeated. He looked at Sara, then at Clint, and then back at Sara. Pointing to Clint, he said, "This is the extra security help you hired?"

"Yes."

"Do you know what this man is?"

"I know who he is, Chief—"

"He's a killer!"

"Hey, hey," Clint said, "I haven't killed anybody all day."

"Smart," Stockton said. "This man can't be trusted around gold."

"You said I was a killer," Clint said, chiding him. "You didn't say anything about me being a thief."

"I'll worry about my man, Chief," Sara said.

Clint was impressed by the way she was handling the chief. Maybe it was because he had called her timid at breakfast.

"Your man," Stockton said derisively.

"Chief, I came here to discuss security arrangements for tomorrow," she said, "and to introduce you to Mr. Adams."

"We've met," Stockton said. "He's not necessary for this meeting."

"Chief—"

"No, Sara," Clint said, "he's right. The security arrangements here in town are up to you and him. I'll get involved once we leave town."

Sara looked at him and then said, "If you're sure . . ."

"Yeah, I'm sure," Clint said. "It was a pleasure to see you again, Chief. I'm looking forward to working with you." He looked at Sara and said, "I'm going to take a look at the train station."

"All right," she said. "I'll see you later."

Stockton didn't say anything until Clint was out the door.

"You must be crazy . . ." Clint heard him say, and then closed the door behind him.

Clint looked at Officer Pressman, who was seated at his desk, and said, "Your chief is a pretty tough character, huh?"

"Sometimes."

"He seems to be pretty rough on you."

The young man made a face.

"I just can't remember to knock every time I go into his office. He doesn't like to be caught—"

"Caught? Doing what?"

"I shouldn't say—"

"Considering how vain your chief appears to be," Clint said, hazarding a guess, "I'd say he had a mirror in his top drawer. Is that it?"

Pressman grinned and nodded.

"He doesn't like to be caught looking at himself in it," the officer said. "That's why he gets angry when I go in without knocking."

"I see," Clint said. "Well, I'd say you better work on remembering."

"Yeah, I know."

"See you . . ."

Clint went to the door, then turned and asked, "Which way to the train station?"

"Make a left when you go out and keep walking. You'll come to it."

"Thanks."

Clint went out, made the left, and kept walking.

It wasn't unusual that the train station was deserted. Without a train there was no reason for anyone to be around. The only soul there was the ticket agent, and Clint went up to the window to talk to him.

"How are you?" he said.

The man looked up and frowned, trying to decide if he knew Clint or not. The agent was an elderly man in his sixties, with snow-white hair and a scrawny chicken neck.

"Mornin'," he said finally.

"Say, how often does the train roll in here?"

"Come in here every six hours."

"Six hours," Clint said. "Starting when?"

"Eight A.M."

"Stopping when?"

"Eight P.M."

"Just two trains a day?"

"That's all."

It wouldn't be hard for someone to figure out which train the gold was on—if they knew which day it was coming. To do that— to know anything—they'd have to have a man on the inside.

Yesterday Sara told Chief Stockton about the gold, and the same evening Clint finds someone following him, maybe with the intention of killing him to get him out of the way.

Why kill him? Why not kill Sara? She'd be an easier target.

Maybe they hadn't thought of that yet. Maybe they wanted to get him out of the way first, and then Sara.

But what about Stockton and his men?

"Hey, Pop?"

The ticket agent looked at him slowly and said, "I ain't your pop."

"Sorry about that. What's your name?"

"Casey."

"Well, Casey, do you know anything about the Police Department?"

"Of course I do, ya blamed fool," Casey said. "I live here, don't I?"

"How many men on the police force?"

"Nine, not counting the chief."

"Ten men altogether."

"Congratulations," the old man said. "Ya can add."

"Yeah, I can," Clint said.

He could subtract, too. With one man on the inside, that left the chief with eight men to guard the gold.

The question was, how many men did the ninth man have to help him?

"Hey, Casey?"

"Ya think I got nothin' to do all day but talk to you?" Casey demanded.

Clint took out a couple of dollars and said, "Sell me a ticket to New York."

"This train don't go to New York, ya damn fool!"

Clint grinned at the man and said, "How do I know that?"

The old man stared at him, then grinned a gap-toothed grin and said, "Maybe ya ain't such a fool after all." The money disappeared into the old man's bony hand.

"So?" he asked.

"Where else does the train stop before it gets here?" Clint asked.

"There's a water stop a couple of miles uptrack," Casey said.

"Does it always stop there?"

"Yep."

"On the way in, or on the way out?"

"Either, or."

"Who decides?"

"The engineer."

"Why there?"

"Why where?"

Patiently Clint said, "Why wasn't the water stop built in town?"

"I didn't build the blamed thing," Casey said. "I just work here."

"Yeah," Clint said, turning away from the window, "me, too."

Chapter Eleven

Clint was standing across the street from the police building when Sara Jones came out. She saw him and crossed over to him.

"Why'd you leave?" she asked.

"You didn't need me in there," he said. "Besides, I wanted to take a look at the train station."

"What'd you see?"

"Not much. A lot of track leading nowhere. There's an old-timer selling tickets who was willing to talk for the price of one."

"About what?"

"Train schedules and stops," Clint said. "If he was willing to talk to me, I bet he'd be willing to talk to anybody."

"What are you saying?"

"If somebody knows about the gold, they got the information from in there," Clint said, pointing to the building across the street. "And they'd be able to get information about the train from old Casey. All they'd have to do then is get me—and you— but of the way."

"What about the chief and his men?"

"Maybe they're not worried about the chief and his men," Clint said.

"Wait a minute," Sara said, frowning. "Are you saying the chief is after the gold? He didn't even know about it until last night."

"And last night I picked up a tail," Clint reminded her.

"Coincidence?"

"If you believe in them."

"And you don't?"

"No."

"What do you believe in, Clint?"

"Are we getting personal again?"

"Curious."

"Hold on to that curiosity" Clint said. "How about some coffee?"

"Didn't you have enough at breakfast?"

"I drink whiskey and beer in moderation," he said. "Coffee I drink to excess."

"Be careful, Clint," Sara said, "that's a piece of personal information."

"Oops," Clint said with a straight face, "it slipped out."

"What do we do now?"

The man called Teddy looked at both of them.

"We wait for a shot."

"Tonight?"

"Yes, tonight, what do you think? Tomorrow's the big day, isn't it?"

"Sure, Teddy—"

"Then get rid of them tonight."

"Them?"

"Adams and the girl."

"Both of them?" one of them said.

"The girl, too?" the other one said.

"What's the matter, you fellas goin' deaf or something?" Teddy asked. "You ain't gettin' paid enough for this?"

The two men exchanged looks, and then one of them said, "Sure, Teddy, we're gettin' paid enough."

"Then do the goddamned job!" Teddy snapped. "Tonight!"

"Are you trying to frighten me?" Sara Denise Jones asked. "Because if you are, you're doing a very good job of it."

"I'm trying to make you aware, that's all," Clint said. "My guess is they meant to take care of me last night and you tonight. Since that didn't work, they'll probably try for both of us tonight."

For a moment he saw panic in her eyes and her lower lip quivered.

"They never told you at Wells Fargo that this job might be dangerous?" he asked, picking up his coffee cup and looking at her over it.

"I knew—I knew there could be so-some danger," she stammered over her own cup. She saw that her hand was shaking and hurriedly put the cup down. She folded her hands in her lap.

"So? Here it is," he said. "The danger has arrived. Don't look so surprised."

"Surprised?" she asked. "Is that what I look? I would have thought I looked more like I was . . . frightened out of my wits."

He stared at her for a moment and then said, "You can handle it."

"I can?"

He nodded and said, "Sure you can."

The look of panic left her eyes and she firmed up her jaw.

"What do we do about it?"

"We stick very close to one another tonight."

She frowned and said, "How close?"

His eyes bore into hers and he said, "*Very* close."

"Now you *are* trying to frighten me," she said, picking up her cup. "When you say close you don't mean . . . sleeping in the same room, do you?"

"Can you get any closer than that?"

"Well, sure," she said. "I mean, we could sleep in the same . . . uh, listen, I hope you don't—"

"We're never going to get anywhere if you constantly think I'm after your . . . virtue," he said, interrupting her. "Can you fire a gun?"

"Of course I can fire a gun."

"Do you have one?"

"Not on me."

"At the office?"

"Yes."

Clint waved the waitress over and said, "Let's go over there. I want to take a look at it."

"Why?"

He stared at her and said, "I want to make sure that if I do get amorous, it'll be big enough to stop me."

Chapter Twelve

"Pressman!"

"Yes, sir?" Officer Pressman said, entering the chief's office.

"I want the men gathered here in one hour."

"All of the men on duty, sir?"

"*All* of the men, Pressman," Stockton said. "Didn't I make myself clear?"

"Yes, sir," Pressman said. "All of the men. I'll have to go out and contact the off-duty men at their—"

"Don't tell me about it," Stockton said. "Go and do it."

"Yes, sir," Pressman said. "I'm on my way, sir."

Stockton closed the door to his office and sat behind his desk. For want of something better to do he pulled out his hand mirror.

It would be nice when he could afford one more ornate.

"Where is it?"

"In the desk drawer," Sara said. "I'll get it."

She went behind the desk, unlocked it with a key, and opened a bottom drawer. From it she took a Colt New Line .22 pistol and held it out for Clint to look at.

"Where did you get this?"

"It was a gift."

His eyebrows went up and he said, "From a gentleman friend?"

"From my uncle."

"I see."

"Why, isn't it any good?"

"As long as you can hit what you aim at, any gun is good enough," he said. "Can you?"

She took it back and said, "Generally. My uncle was a very good shot, and he taught me how to shoot."

"Good. Carry it with you at all times."

She picked up her purse and put the gun in it.

"Now tell me about the plans you and the chief made."

"Very simple, really," she said. "He intends to have his full complement of men at the station."

"Really? All nine, eh?"

"Yes, plus himself."

"And us," he said. "That makes twelve. How many men does your company have on the train?"

"Two."

"Just two?"

"They didn't want to be conspicuous."

"How would they like to be responsible for losing a quarter of a million dollars?"

"They were going to be very secretive," she said. "Nobody knows that the gold is on the train."

"Except us, and the chief, and everyone in his department, by now."

Suddenly she put her hands up to her mouth.

"You mean . . . I told him about it too soon? If that gold is stolen it'll be my—"

"Your responsibility," Clint said, cutting her short, "but not your fault. You were right to inform the local police."

"But I could have waited until today," she said. "If Stockton—or one of his men—is after the gold, I gave them enough time to come up with some kind of a plan."

"You could look at it that way."

"You don't?"

"I just naturally expect someone to try to steal it," he said. "That way I'm ready for anything."

"I suppose that's a better way to look at it."

"Let's take a ride."

"Where?"

"Two miles uptrack," he said. "I want to have a look at the water stop."

"I'll have to change," she said.

He looked at her shirt and pants and said, "What's wrong with what you have on?"

She looked at him like he was crazy and said, "I have to change into riding clothes."

"Okay, fine," he said. "I'll come with you."

"Come with me?"

"We've got to stay close to each other, remember?" he said. "I can help you with hard-to-get-at buttons."

"On second thought," she said, "I can ride dressed like this."

"I'm sure you can."

"It's a water tower," she said.

"I can see that."

They were each astride their horses, staring up at the water tower.

"What did you expect to see?" she asked.

"Nothing," he said, "and everything."

"Why do you speak in riddles?"

"I only do that when I have no answers," he said, dismounting. He handed her the reins.

"Where are you going?"

"I'm going to climb up and look inside," he called back.

"Well, don't fall in," she shouted. "I can't come in after you, because I can't swim."

"Neither can I . . ."

She watched as Clint ascended the ladder to the top of the tower and looked inside. Apparently satisfied with what he saw, he came back down.

What he saw was water, and unless someone was underwater, holding his or her breath, there was no one inside. Of course, that didn't mean there wouldn't be anyone inside when the train stopped there.

Of course, if it stopped on its way out, it wouldn't make a difference.

If, however, it stopped on the way in . . .

When he returned she handed him back his reins and he mounted up.

"Sara, can you get in touch with the men on the train?" he asked.

"I suppose I can," she said. "They have to stop to let passengers off. I could leave them a message."

"Let's get back to town and do that," he said.

"What do you want me to tell them?"

"Not to let the train stop for water on the way into town," he said. "Then we won't have to worry about anything happening at the water stop."

"That's a good idea."

"Thank you."

"I think I hired the right man for the job," she went on, "despite what Chief Stockton said about you."

He looked at her and she said, "Well, you heard part of it."

"Yeah," he said, "he called me a killer."

She laughed and said, "And that was the nicest thing he said about you."

Chapter Thirteen

It was afternoon when they got back to town. They left their horses at the livery and then walked to the telegraph office.

As they entered, the operator let out a loud curse, then looked up and saw Sara.

"Oh, excuse me, miss."

"That's all right."

"What's the problem?" Clint asked.

"Goldang thing's gone on the fritz," the man said. He looked like he could be the ticket taker's brother. Same white hair and scrawny neck, same bony hands. This one seemed to have more teeth, though.

"What's wrong with it?" Clint asked.

"Damned if I know."

"Can you fix it?"

"If I knew what was wrong with it maybe I could fix it," he said.

"Well, what *could* be wrong with it?"

"Could be a line down," the operator said.

"And if that's the case?"

"Then somebody'd have to shinny up a pole and reconnect it."

"Can you do that?"

"Sonny," the man said, eyeing Clint with obvious disregard for his intelligence, "do I look spry enough to you to go shinnying up poles?"

"And if I called you Pop, you probably would get mad at me," Clint said. "There's no pleasing you old-timers."

"We can refer to our age and use it as an excuse," the man said.

"Curmudgeon," Clint said.

"What?"

"I said I understand that," Clint said. "Can you have someone ride out and check the wires? We'd like to send an important message."

"Everybody's message is important, sonny," the man said. "Well, I'll have to close up and ride the line with Ethan."

"Who's Ethan?"

"Young fella I use to shinny up poles," the man said. "He climbs, and I tell him what to do."

"Sounds like a perfect partnership."

"It would be, if Ethan had any brains."

"I could ride out with you," Clint offered.

"You'll excuse me, mister," the old man said, "but I don't know you. I'd just as soon ride out with Ethan."

"Suit yourself."

"I usually do," he said. "Would you mind leaving? I got to lock up."

Clint and Sara left. Behind them the old man locked the office and then went off to look for Ethan.

"Well, who knows how long it will take for him and Ethan to get it fixed," she said.

"Probably just long enough," Clint said.

"You sound like you think somebody may have deliberately damaged the line."

"It's a distinct possibility, Sara."

"Then we're isolated," she said, "with only a police force we can't trust to help us."

"That's the way it looks."

"So what do we do now?"

He looked at her and said, "How about a cup of coffee?"

"Just how much coffee do you drink during the course of a day?"

"I never stop."

"To count?"

"No," he said, "I never stop drinking it."

"Well, I do," she said.

"Then you can watch me drink it," he said, "or you can drink tea, because where I go, you go."

Suddenly she looked around and asked, "Do you think they're watching us right now?"

"Yes."

"I wonder where they are."

"Across the street, in the doorway of the hardware store— don't look!"

"If you know where they are, how can they just stand there and watch us?"

"They don't know I know," he said. "*They* think they're following us without our knowledge."

"How did you see them?"

"I make it my business never to be followed without knowing it," he said. "It's healthier. How about that coffee?"

"Whatever you say, Clint."

Chapter Fourteen

Clint and Sara spent the rest of the afternoon together, and then had dinner at the same café where they'd eaten the day before.

"Are they still following us?" she asked as they sat down.

"One or the other has been with us the whole time," Clint said.

"Well, what are we supposed to do about it?" she asked. "Just let them follow us until they decide to try to kill us?"

"Yes."

"What?" she said. "What do you mean, 'yes'?"

"I can't very well attack them just for following us. Stockton would never stand for that."

"So you're going to wait until they try to kill you to do something? That's crazy."

"Listen, these two are inept at best, Sara," Clint said. "If they try to kill me they'll probably just get in each other's way."

"Why didn't you do something yesterday, then?"

"Last night I didn't know they were incompetent," he said. "I only suspected it."

"And now you know it?"

"Definitely," Clint said. "Tonight we'll question one of them about who he works for."

"And the other one?"

"We'll . . . do something about him."

"Not kill him," she said firmly. "I won't stand for that, Clint."

"Sara—"

"I'm sorry, but I have to be firm about this, Clint," Sara said. "My company would be very unhappy—"

"Are you're putting your foot down on this?" he asked her.

She thought it over and then said, "Uh . . . yes, I am."

"All right."

"All right . . . what?"

"I won't kill one of them . . ."

"Good."

" . . . as long as I don't have to."

"Who decides if you have to or not?"

"I do."

"Wait—"

"Do you want to order?" Clint asked as the waiter came over to the table.

"Uh, bring me the stew," she said.

"Yeah," Clint said, "the stew. Two of them."

"Yes, sir."

As the man left, Sara leaned forward and said in a low voice, "What makes it so easy for you to talk about killing someone?"

"Because I've done it before," Clint said.

"And it's easy?"

"Look, Sara—"

"If this is too personal, I'm sorry," she said, cutting him off, "but I feel very strongly about this."

He studied her for a moment and saw that on this point she was not going to back down. He wondered for a moment if what she was paying him was worth all of this shit.

"It's not easy to kill, Sara," Clint said. "In fact, it's damn hard, but often there's just no other way."

"It's necessary."

"That's right."

"Well, I'm sorry, but I just don't think that killing is necessary—I mean, unless you're in danger of being killed yourself."

"And what are we talking about here?"

"We don't *know* that those two men *are* going to try to kill us," she said, "and you're talking about killing one just so we can question the other."

"Wait a minute," he said. "What do you mean 'we'?"

"Well, I'll be there—"

"No, you won't."

"Yes, I will," she said. "You're the one who said it. Where you go I go."

Clint stared at her, wondering where the timid soul who'd come looking for him in San Francisco had gone. This girl was turning out to be one of the stubbornest people he'd met in a while.

"You do remember saying that?"

"Sure I do, but that was for your protection," Clint said.

"And tonight you're going to leave me unprotected while you go looking for those two men?"

"Once I isolate them, you'll be in no danger."

"What does that mean, 'isolate'?"

"You know, I'd swear you have two different personalities," Clint said. "What happened to that sweet, shy—"

"If I have two different personalities, then you bring the other one out in me," she said. "I'm not the only one, though."

"What do you mean?"

"You have two personalities, too."

"Me?"

"Sure. There's the man who earlier today made me feel as if I could handle anything that comes along, and then . . ."

"And then?"

"And then there's the man who talks about killing the way other people talk about . . . about gardening."

"I'm a very good gardener," Clint said.

"Clint—"

"Here comes dinner," Clint said. "How about we use our mouths to eat, and nothing else?"

"I have a sneaking suspicion you're telling me to shut up."

"Not at all," Clint said. "Eat."

"Jesus, I'm hungry," Paul Spikes said.

"So am I," Lee Burke said, "but only one of us can go and get something to eat while the other one keeps an eye on them."

Spikes and Burke were the two men who had been watching Clint and Sara all day, as they had been instructed to by Teddy.

"So which one of us eats?" Spikes asked.

"I don't know," Burke said. "If one of us leaves the other, the chance we've been waiting for might come. If that happens and we miss it, we won't get paid."

"If what Teddy said about Clint Adams is true, I don't think I want to try to take him alone," Spikes said.

"I know," Burke said. "I feel the same way. I heard about the Gunsmith. He's supposed to be faster than Hickok was."

"So why are we going to try at all?" Spikes asked.

"For money," Burke said. "The same reason we do everything."

"Yeah," Spikes said.

Both men settled down to watch the café, wishing they were in it.

Chapter Fifteen

"I'll bet you'd like a drink," Sara said.

They hadn't talked much through dinner, and she'd watched him consume a potful of coffee afterward. Now they were walking . . . just walking, because Clint didn't know where to go with Sara Denise Jones in tow.

"What?" he said.

"A drink," Sara said. "Don't you usually have a drink after dinner?"

"Sometimes . . ."

"Well, what about tonight?" she said. "There's a saloon right across the street."

"So there is."

"You're not stopping."

"I think we'd be better off if we got indoors."

"The saloon is indoors, Clint."

"Sara, maybe I don't want a drink tonight."

She grabbed his arm and stopped his progress.

"Maybe you just don't want to go into the saloon with me."

"You don't belong in a saloon, Sara."

"Why not?"

"Because you're a woman."

"I happen to know that women occasionally work in saloons."

"Those aren't women, they're . . . saloon girls."

"Saloon girls aren't women?"

"I didn't mean that . . ."

"Come on," she said, stepping into the street. "I'll buy you a drink."

"Sara—"

"I'm going in for a drink, with or without you . . ." she called out, continuing across the street.

Clint shook his head and started after her.

"They're going into the saloon," Burke said.

"I can see that," Spikes said.

"What do we do?"

"We wait for them to come out," Spikes said. "This could be our chance, Burke."

Both men took out their guns, checked them, and then holstered them.

Clint caught up to Sara just before she entered the saloon, and they walked in together.

"Just stay by me," he said.

Nervously she said, "I'm not going anywhere."

They walked to the bar, and Clint ordered two beers.

The saloon was full, and Sara—being the only woman in the place other than the saloon girls—attracted a lot of attention.

Clint saw both Candy and Darleen looking his way, and hoped neither one of them would approach him.

"I've never been in a saloon before," Sara said.

"And you shouldn't be in this one."

"I can't help it," she said. "For some reason you bring out the stubborn in me."

He was about to reply when he saw Darleen headed his way.

"Friend of yours?" Sara asked.

"Acquaintance."

"Ah-ha," Sara said, and busied herself with her beer as Darleen reached them.

"New friend?" Darleen asked.

"Acquaintance," Clint said.

"I see," Darleen said. "I guess that means you won't be staying tonight?"

"I've got other plans, Darleen."

"So I see," Darleen said, looking past him at Sara. "If you change your mind, let me know."

Clint looked at Sara and saw her looking at Darleen, inspecting her. He decided to finish his beer and get her out of there.

"Finished?" he asked, putting his empty mug down.

"I still have half a beer left," she pointed out. "Why don't you have another?"

"I told you once before," he said. "I drink in moderation."

Across the room a man reached out, put his arm around Darleen's waist, and pulled her to him.

"Let go, Earl," she snapped at him.

"Come on, Darleen," the man said. "That fella ain't interested in you, but I am."

"Earl, let go!"

"Come on, Darleen, honey," Earl said. He put one hand on one of her breasts and squeezed.

"Ow!"

"Are you going to stand there and watch?" Sara asked.

Clint had been watching, and now he turned his head to look at Sara.

"You're right," he said. "Let's leave."

"That's not what I mean!" she said, putting her beer mug down with a bang. "Go and help her."

"She doesn't need any help."

"That man is pawing her!"

"She gets paid to be pawed," Clint pointed out.

"Earl, damn it!" Darleen shouted. "You're hurtin' me!"

"See?" Sara said.

"Sara, if you're finished with your beer—"

"I can't believe you!" she said, and stalked across the room to where Earl was holding Darleen in his lap, trying to kiss her.

"Let her go!" Sara shouted at him.

The man looked at her and said with a broad smile, "Take it easy, sweetie. You came in with your man. Darleen here is gonna get hers."

"She doesn't want you, mister," Sara said, "so let her go!"

"Look," Earl said, getting annoyed, "mind your own damned business."

"It's all right," Darleen said while squirming. "Really, I can handle it."

"You can't even get loose," Sara said. "Look at this man, he's three times your size."

"I'm enough man for both of you, if you're interested, sweetheart," Earl said with a leer.

Sara turned and glared furiously at Clint, who shrugged.

"Damn men!" Sara shouted.

The men in the place were laughing as Sara stormed toward the batwing doors and out into the darkness.

Earl released Darleen, who stood up, smoothing her dress out.

"What's wrong with her?" he asked.

Clint moved to the doors and stepped outside.

"There's the woman," Burke said.

"She's alone," Spikes said.

"Now's our chance," Burke said.

"What about the man?"

"We can get him later," Burke said. "Let's get her *now*."

Clint saw the two men rush from their doorway, and his first instinct was to hurry after Sara, but then he held back.

This was the chance he'd been waiting for, to bring them out into the open, making a move he could oppose, and not have to worry about explaining it to the law afterward.

Chapter Sixteen

Sara Denise had left the saloon so quickly that she hadn't thought about the consequences. Now, as she walked the street alone, after dark, she realized what she had done.

But it was Clint who had made her do it. He'd gotten her so angry by not trying to help that girl!

Sara had a room behind her office, and that was where she was headed. To get to the room, though, she had to go down an alley, and at this time of night the alley would be like midnight without a moon.

She turned, with intentions of returning to the saloon for Clint, and that was when she saw the two men.

Damn him, he'd made her mad enough to rush out into the street to her own death. She was sure the two men were going to kill her.

She reached into her purse for the Colt New Line and held it in her hand. She had fired the gun before, but she had never fired it *at* anyone. She didn't even know if she could fire at another human being.

Maybe, she thought, if it was that or die.

She quickened her pace, trying to reach her office before the men could reach her, and then she was running, and she knew they were running behind her.

She ran with grace and ease. She knew she was a

fast runner, but how long could she stay ahead of the two men? Eventually they would catch her if she didn't reach her room first.

She glanced behind her once and saw that they were closing on her. She didn't know what to do. Panic rose within her. Should she scream, or just turn and fire at them?

What would Clint do?

That was easy.

He'd kill them.

Panic and adrenaline gave her more speed, and finally she came to the alley next to her office. As she turned into it a pair of hands grabbed her and held her fast.

"No!" she cried, trying to bring the gun to bear.

"Easy," Clint said. "It's me."

"Clint!"

"Slow down," he told her. "We'll lose them."

"Lose them?"

"Let them follow you into the alley," he whispered. "I'll do the rest."

Suddenly he melted into the darkness and was gone. She remembered that there was a doorway in the alley other than hers. He had obviously slipped into it.

She turned and saw the men catching up to her again. She waited until they were almost on her, then turned and ran into the alley.

She hurried to the other end, and as she reached the door to her room, she heard sounds of a struggle. Instead of entering, she waited there, listening. . . .

After a moment someone came toward her. Panic threatened to make her run, but she held fast and finally saw Clint moving toward her, dragging a man behind him.

"Is he . . ."

"Dead?" Clint said. "No, he's unconscious."

"And his friend?"

"The same."

"You didn't kill him?"

"No, damn it!"

"Shall we take him inside?"

"No," Clint said. "Go inside, leave the door open, and light a lamp."

She did as she was told, and the light from the lamp filtered out into the alley.

Clint leaned over the man and slapped his face, bringing him to.

"What's your name?" he asked.

"What happened?"

"Never mind," Clint said. He took his gun out and pressed it to the man's nostril.

"What's your name?"

"B-B-Burke!"

"Why were you following me and the lady all day?"

"F-f-following?"

"Don't try my patience," Clint said, pressing the gun barrel harder into his face. "I know you've been follow-ing me for two days. Why?"

"I can't—"

"Look out!" Sara shouted.

Clint turned in time to see the other man standing over him. He'd left him unconscious at the other end of the alley, his gun thrown into the darkness, but somehow the man had found it.

He should have killed him!

Clint pushed off with his legs and tumbled backward just as the man fired. He heard a grunt of pain, but had no time to see if it was the man or Sara who had been hit. He turned his gun on the standing man and fired. His muzzle flash lit the alley, and he saw the man fall.

Quickly he got to his feet to check the other man—and Sara.

"Sara!"

"Here," her voice came from inside. She peeked out and asked, "Are you all right?"

"Yes. You?"

"Fine," she said. "What about them?"

Clint checked both men and found them both dead. The man he had shot had accidently killed his partner when Clint had ducked away. The killing shot had been meant for him.

"They're both dead."

"You killed them?"

"I killed that one," he said, pointing. "He killed his own man trying to kill me."

She stared at the two men for a moment, by the light filtering out of her room.

"Come inside . . ." she said, reaching for him.

"No," he said. "Let's get away from here."

"And go where?"

"My hotel."

"But why? We can—"

"Look, Sara," he said, "Stockton is just bastard enough to use this to lock me away. We've got to go to my hotel and give him the same story."

"What story?"

"That while your office was broken into, you and I were in my room."

"Together?"

"Together."

"Doing what?"

Clint grabbed her arm and said, "Whatever the chief wants to think we were doing. The point is we weren't here. Understand?"

"I understand."

"Then let's go, before one of Stockton's men responds to the shots."

Clint dragged her with him out the other end of the alley, and then to his hotel.

Chapter Seventeen

When the knock came at the door, Sara was lying on the bed, and Clint was sitting in the chair. Neither of them had fallen asleep.

"Adams, open the door, damn you!"

"Stockton," she whispered.

"Get under the covers," Clint said, quickly removing his shirt. "I'm going to open the door and let him see you."

"Do you think he's going to believe this?" she asked, sliding under the covers.

Clint reached for her shirt and pulled it down past her shoulders, so they were bare. He popped two buttons in the process.

Clint's holster was hanging on the bedpost, and he took his gun from it.

"He'll believe it now," Clint said. He'd removed his boots immediately upon arriving in the room, and now he walked to the door in his socks.

"Adams!" Stockton yelled again.

When he opened it he held the gun down at his side.

"What the hell—" Stockton started, but he stopped when Clint moved just enough so that the police chief could see over his shoulder, to Sara in the bed. Pressman was by his side, and he leaned over to look in as well.

73

All they could both see were her bare shoulders above the blankets.

"What is it, Clint?" she called out, contriving to sound sleepy.

"It's the chief," Clint said over his shoulder.

"Is something wrong?" she asked.

"Is there something wrong, Chief?" Clint asked.

"Have the two of you been here all night?" Stockton asked.

"All night?" Clint repeated. "Well, since after dinner, yes. Why?"

"Someone tried to break into Miss Jones's office," Stockton said.

"My office?" she said. She sat up in the bed but kept the sheet pulled up to her shoulders. "What happened? Did they get into the safe?"

"Two men tried to break in," Stockton said. "They're both dead."

"Dead?" Clint said. "You got them, then."

"No," Stockton said. "They were dead when I got there. Someone shot them."

"Who?" Clint asked.

"I don't know that," Stockton said, and it pained him to admit it. "It's strange. From the way it looked, one of them might have killed the other."

"Maybe one of them broke in and the other tried to stop him, and they killed each other?" Clint suggested.

"I doubt it," Stockton said. "I've seen those two around town and they've always been together."

"I'll have to go and lock up," Sara said, making as if to rise.

"There's no need for that," Chief Stockton said. "The safe wasn't broken into, and I've had my men secure the premises."

"We appreciate that, Chief," Clint said.

Stockton gave Clint a withering look, and Sara a pitying one. Obviously he felt that she could have done better for herself.

"If you'll come by my office in the morning, Miss Jones, we'll go to *your* office together." He was ignoring Clint at this point. "If anything is missing, you can let me know."

"All right, Chief," Sara said. "I appreciate your help."

"From there we'll go to the station and wait for the train."

"Fine," Clint said.

He gave them both one last look and then turned away so quickly he collided with Pressman, who was still trying to see beneath Sara's sheet. He pushed the younger officer down the hall and followed.

Clint closed the door and turned to look at Sara, who had released the sheet. Beneath it she was still fully clothed.

"It might have been more convincing if you had showed him a little shoulder, at least."

"You wish," she said.

She gave him a look that surprised him—one he could only term "saucy"—and turned over to go to sleep.

Chapter Eighteen

In the morning Clint woke stiff from sleeping sitting up in the chair all night. When he opened his eyes Sara was lying awake in bed, propped up on one elbow, watching him.

"What's wrong?"

"Nothing," she said.

He sat up and stretched, trying to work out the stiffness.

"How do you feel?" she asked. "You look more than a little stiff."

"I'm fine," he said.

He looked out the window and saw that it was not yet fully light.

"What time's the train coming in again? Eight?" he asked.

"Yes."

"And the stage that will take the gold from there?" That was something he should have asked long ago.

"I should have told you before," she said, sitting up and putting her feet on the floor. She was still fully dressed, having removed nothing but her boots.

"The stage is here already," she explained. "It's behind the livery. The two men who are accompanying the gold on the train will drive it to Los Angeles from there."

"I see," he said. "And then we'll ride along with them?"

She didn't answer right away.

"Well?"

"I hadn't thought about going along," she said. "I thought I'd see them off, and that would be the end of my job."

"Isn't it your responsibility to see that the gold *gets* to Los Angeles?"

"I guess it is," she said.

"You'd better do more than guess," Clint said, pushing painfully to his feet. "I want to know exactly when my job ends."

She started to answer but he waved her off, saying, "You've got time. Just be ready to let me know after we off-load the gold."

She nodded and said, "All right."

"Now we'd better go over to the chief's office—and remember to smile a lot."

"Smile?" she asked. "Why?"

"You've just spent the night with me, haven't you?"

She stuck her tongue out at him and picked up her boots.

Stockton was waiting for them at his office. He gave them and their disheveled looks a disapproving look, then accompanied them to the Wells Fargo office. Sara gave the place a search for the chief's benefit and pronounced nothing missing.

"We might as well get over to the train station, then," the chief said. "My men should be there already."

When they reached the train station Stockton's men—in uniform—were milling about. When they saw him the ones who were sitting stood, the ones who were leaning stood, and the ones who were slouching stood.

"Nice-looking bunch," Clint said.

"You don't look like someone who should be commenting on someone else's looks," Stockton said stiffly.

"What *do* I look like?"

"A man who spent the night in a chair."

Clint couldn't argue that point—and even if he could have, he wouldn't have, because it would have exposed their lie about spending the night together.

"Let's take a look around," Clint said. "It's almost eight."

Stockton went to confer with his men while Clint looked the station over. Other than the chief, his men, Sara, and himself, the only other soul around was the old ticket taker, Casey.

"Doesn't look like anyone else is coming in on this train," Clint said to Sara. "Wells Fargo hasn't taken the entire train, have they?"

"No."

"And there's no one here to greet the arrivals?" he asked.

"Maybe there's no one coming in," she said, "or maybe if there are people coming in, there's no one here to meet them. Either way, we don't have to worry about anyone else hanging around to see the gold."

"Yeah," he said, "there is that."

They found a bench and sat down to wait. At five past eight Clint went over to talk to the ticket taker.

"Is this train usually on time?"

"Always."

"Except now."

The old man looked at his watch and said, "Yep, except now. Well, there's always a first time, ya know."

"Yeah, I know."

Clint went back to sit next to Sara.

At eight-fifteen he looked around and counted Stockton's men.

"Nine," he said, standing up.

"What?" Sara asked.

"There are nine men here."

"That's how many he's supposed to have."

"Yeah, but somebody should be out at that water tower," he said. "That asshole has kept all of his men here."

Clint found Stockton and confronted him.

"You didn't put any men at the water tower?"

"Why should I have?" the chief asked. "The gold is being unloaded here."

"But if the train stops for water, that's the ideal place to hit them."

"If anyone knows about the gold," Stockton said.

"Oh, someone knows," Clint said.

"Who?" Stockton asked. "And how would they?"

"You tell me," Clint said and turned away.

"Wait!"

Clint stopped and turned to face the older man.

"What?"

"Are you accusing me of having a . . . a thief in my department?"

"I didn't accuse you of anything."

"You implied—"

"If you heard an implication in what I said, that's your problem, Stockton."

"Where are you going?" Stockton demanded as Clint started away again.

"I'm riding out to the water tower," Clint said. "That train is almost twenty minutes late."

"I'm coming with you," Sara said.

"So am I," Stockton said. "I want to be there when you find nothing."

"Let's go," Clint told them both. "It may already be too late."

Chapter Nineteen

Clint, Sara, and Stockton rode up the line, and the closer they got to the water tower, the more convinced Clint became that something had gone wrong. He could yell and scream at Stockton all he wanted that he hadn't put any men on the water tower, but if he'd had any sense at all he would have gone out there himself.

When the water tower finally came into view, the train was sitting still right next to it.

"Shit," Clint said to himself. He looked at Sara and said, "It's been hit!"

"We don't know that for sure," Stockton said.

"It's a pretty damn safe bet."

They rode up on the train and dismounted. Clint tried the engine first and found the engineer and fireman tied and gagged. The fireman must have gotten brave and had his head busted open for him, but it had stopped bleeding and he seemed all right.

Sara climbed up into the engine after him and Clint said, "Untie them. I'll check on your men."

He dropped down from the engine and started on back, looking for the car where the gold must have been kept.

"What's going on?" Stockton demanded, coming up behind him.

"The engineer and fireman were tied up. Let's find the car— there it is."

He knew it was the one because the big sliding door was wide open. When he reached the car he climbed inside and found the two Wells Fargo men.

Stockton, whose bulk kept him from climbing in after him, called out, "Well? What's happening?"

Clint came to the open door and looked down at the chief.

"They're both dead."

"And the gold?"

Clint dropped down to the ground and said, "The gold is gone."

"What happened to the men?"

"They were shot."

Stockton looked around, as if he expected to see a clue somewhere nearby to what happened.

Looking up the line, Clint saw that some of the passengers had gotten out of the train and were coming toward them.

"Chief, why don't you deal with those people while I go and talk to the engineer and fireman."

"Why should I deal with them?" Stockton asked belligerently.

"Because you're the representative of the law around here, and you're the one they're going to want to see, not me."

Clint didn't wait for the chief to agree. He turned and headed for the engine.

When he climbed back in the engine, Sara had both men untied, and she and the engineer were examining the fireman's head.

"How is he?"

"He'll be fine," Sara said. "He needs a doctor, but he'll be fine."

"What happened here?" Clint asked the engineer.

"We were flagged down, and when we stopped, the roof fell in," the man replied.

"How many were there?"

"Two men up here," he said. "I don't know how many otherwise. Did they get anything?"

"Yes," Clint said. "A Wells Fargo gold shipment."

"I was afraid of that," the engineer said.

"What about the . . . the men?" Sara asked.

"They're dead," he said. The news hit her like a slap in the face. He supposed he should have sugarcoated it somehow, but that just wasn't something he was used to doing.

"Dead?"

"Shot," he said, nodding.

"I want to see."

"See what?" he asked.

"I should see."

"There's nothing to see—"

She turned and climbed down from the engine, and he followed.

"Five cars up," he said.

She was walking fast, and as she approached the car she began to run. When she reached it she couldn't climb into it.

"Help me!"

He put both hands on her butt and pushed her up into the car. He waited outside for her, watching the chief do his best to calm the passengers down.

He heard a sharp gasp from inside and turned as she came to the door. Her eyes were wet.

"Help me down, please."

He reached up for her and lowered her to the ground gently.

"Could we have prevented this?" she asked.

"Maybe . . ."

"Adams?"

Clint turned to look at Stockton.

"This isn't my fault, you know."

"Sure," Clint said.

"It's mine," Sara said.

"Sure," Clint said in the same tone of voice.

To Stockton he said, "What did the passengers tell you?"

"They saw two men," Stockton said. "They held them all in the passenger car."

"Was anything taken from the passengers?"

"No. They were told to stay in the car for one hour, or they'd be shot. They didn't move until we arrived."

Clint looked at Sara and said, "I still have some questions for the engineer."

"All right," she said.

The three of them walked back to the engine. By this time the engineer was on the ground, waiting for them. The wounded fireman was probably resting in the engine.

"Why'd you stop?" Clint asked him.

"I told you," the man said. "We got flagged down."

"You didn't stop for water?"

"No."

"Do you usually stop for just anybody who flags you down?"

"Not just anybody, no."

"Then why this time?"

"Because he was a policeman."

"What?" Stockton demanded.

The engineer looked at Stockton and said, "The man who flagged us down was a policeman."

"And just how the hell do you know that?" Stockton asked.

Clint, Sara, and Stockton looked at the man expectantly and he said, "Because he was wearing a uniform."

Chapter Twenty

While Stockton argued with the engineer about his eyesight, Clint walked back to the car where the dead Wells Fargo men were.

"Maybe you've got bad eyesight . . ." Stockton was saying to the man.

Sara ran after Clint and grabbed his arm.

"Clint!"

"What?"

"We have to do something."

"Like what?" he asked. He shook off her hand and continued walking.

"We have to get that gold back!"

"Uh-huh."

They reached the car, and Clint started inspecting the ground.

"What are you looking for?"

"That," Clint said, pointing.

"What?"

"Tracks," Clint said. He looked farther and said, "Four men, maybe five."

"Two in the passenger car and two in the engine," she said. "That makes nine."

"Unless the two in the engine came back here after taking care of the engineer and the fireman," Clint said.

"But for the sake of argument we'll say nine—ten if there was one man driving the wagon."

"Wagon?"

He pointed to the tracks the wagon wheels had made.

"They would have needed a wagon to haul that gold," Clint said. He knelt down to study the tracks closer, then stood up. "The tracks are heavier going out than they were coming in."

"Then they do have the gold."

"Somebody's got it," Clint said, "and these tracks are all we've got. I'll have to follow them now, Sara, or they'll get too far ahead of me."

"Us."

"What?"

"I'm going, too."

"Sara, I'm not even outfitted for this," he said. "All I'll have is water."

"We'd better get started," she said. "The longer we wait, the farther away they get."

She was using his own words against him.

"Sara, I'll have to travel fast—"

"I can ride, Clint," she said, "and I can shoot. What else do I have to know how to do?"

He gave her a hard look and said, "Survive."

"You can't do this," Stockton told them.

"Why not?" Sara asked.

"You're not police," he said. "Neither of you has any authority."

"That's Wells Fargo property that's been stolen, Chief Stockton," Sara said. "I have all the authority I need to go after it."

"What about him?" Stockton asked, pointing to Clint, who was already astride his horse, waiting.

"He works for me."

"Adams, if you do this—"

"Talk to the lady, Chief," Clint said, interrupting him. "She's the boss."

"I'll have you both behind bars."

"Fine," Clint said. "Right now you better worry about getting your men here from the station. After that you can follow us."

"Adams—"

"Here come the passengers, Chief," Clint said. "You'd better get them into town pretty quick, too. Might be somebody important on board."

"Can you crank this thing up?" Stockton asked the engineer.

"Sure, Chief."

"Then do it."

He turned to talk to Sara and Clint again, but they had already started following the tracks of the gold thieves.

"Adams! Jones! Come back here!"

Chapter Twenty-One

At that moment the nine men who had stolen the gold stopped to take a look at it. Eight were mounted, while one drove the wagon holding the gold.

"Come on," one of them said, dismounting, "I want to look at it." His name was Healy.

"We should keep moving," another man said. He was called Bishop. A tall, well-built man in his thirties, he had been in charge of the actual theft of the gold, although it had been planned by Teddy.

"Come on, Bishop," one of the other men said. "We can at least take a look at it."

"Get back on your horse, Healy," Bishop said. "We'll look at the gold when Teddy says, and not before."

"He won't even know," Healy said, climbing onto the buckboard. The chest that held the gold had been tied down so it wouldn't shift while they were traveling.

"Healy, I'm warning you," Bishop said.

Bishop had recruited and hired the eight men who were with him, but he worked for the man they all knew as Teddy. None of the men knew if that was his first name or last name, or if it was even his real name. In fact, they knew *of* him, but none of them had ever seen him.

"Take it easy, Bishop," Healy said, standing over the chest. "Don't take it so seriously. Even if the law is on our trail, we've got enough of a head start to stop for a quick peek."

"No peek, Healy," Bishop said. "Follow orders, like everybody else. Nobody gets a look at that gold until we get where we're going."

"And where is that?"

"You'll find that out, too, when the time comes."

"Hey, now look, Bishop—"

Bishop produced his gun faster than the others could follow and pointed it at Healy.

"You were the one I knew I wouldn't be able to trust, Healy," he said, "but I needed eight men. Now I don't need you anymore."

"You wouldn't—"

Bishop fired and the bullet struck Healy in the chest, forcing him back until he fell from the buckboard to the ground.

Bishop looked around at the other seven men and asked, "Does anyone else want to take a peek?"

They all shook their heads to some degree, agreeing that no one wanted to risk facing Pete Bishop's gun just for a look at a quarter of a million dollars in gold.

Not when there was a piece of it waiting for them at the end of the road.

Pete Bishop knew he had made one mistake. There was not one man among these he had recruited that he could talk to or confide in. Therefore he had to keep to himself that their destination was Mexico.

Still, if any of them had half a brain they'd figure that after stealing a fortune in gold the only place they were safe to divvy it up would be Mexico, where U.S. law couldn't touch them.

Bishop had been contacted especially by Teddy, because Bishop was a known thief and gunman. That is, Teddy knew Bishop was a thief and gunman, but also knew that he could be trusted.

Bishop was a professional thief, which meant he had worked— and would work—with other thieves. When he worked with other professionals, they knew they could trust each other, because it defeated the purpose of having "partners" if you had to worry about them trying to kill you or steal your share after the job was done.

It was men like Healy, though, who gave thieving a bad name. Bishop figured Healy would try to kill him the first chance he got, and he wouldn't have put it past these other men to go along with it. Now, however, with their leader dead, they'd fall in line and do what Bishop told them to do—until they picked a new leader, anyway.

Hopefully they wouldn't be able to put anything together until they got to Mexico and met with Teddy.

Still, Bishop wished he had at least one man along he could trust. If this bunch ever did get the backbone to brave him, it'd be one gun against seven.

Bishop needed *one* more man.

Maybe he could pick him up along the way somewhere.

Chapter Twenty-Two

Clint was pushing it, and Sara—even though he knew she was trying—was lagging behind. Clint kept up his pace, though, because sooner or later she'd have to give it up and head back, although already she had come farther than he thought she would.

They'd been riding about four hours now, and the sun was almost directly overhead. It was a hot one, and Clint's shirt was plastered to his body by perspiration. At this point his horse was fairly lathered, too, so when he finally did stop it was to rest the horse, not to let Sara catch up.

When she did catch up he had dismounted and was sitting on a large rock with his canteen in hand.

"Dismount and give that animal some rest," he instructed her.

She did so, taking her canteen with her. Her shirt was soaked through with sweat, and he was somewhat surprised to see that she had no undergarment underneath it. The shapes of her breasts were clearly defined, and he could see the hard points of her nipples clearly. She was firmer and rounder than he would have thought.

She saw him looking at her and lowered her eyes, but a couple of days ago she would have blushed, so maybe she was coming along.

She sat down on the ground and drank some water from her canteen.

"Take it easy with that," Clint said. "It'll be nightfall before we come to water."

"You don't think we'll catch them before nightfall?" she asked wearily.

"Somebody knows what they're doing," he said. "They've been stopping to rest in shifts, and the wagon hasn't stopped at all. If they had thought to bring fresh horses with them, we'd really be in trouble."

"It's not hopeless, though."

"It's never hopeless until you're dead, Sara," he said. "And then who gives a . . . damn?"

"There you go again," she said.

"What?"

"Talking about death. God, but you are so obsessed with death—the death of other people."

"Well, I'd rather that than be obsessed with my own, like most people are."

"Are you saying I'm obsessed with my own death?" she demanded.

"I'm not saying anything of the kind," he said. "Don't be so quick to take offense."

"I'm not taking offense," she said, wiping off her brow with the sleeve of her shirt.

"How *do* you feel about death?"

"I . . . never think about it."

That was a lie. It had been Clint's observation that everyone thinks about his or her own death often, if not all the time. They're so worried they're going to die before they're ready that they spend the time they have worrying about dying.

"Give your horse some of that water," he said, standing up.

"How?"

"Pour it into your hat," he said, "but don't give him too much."

He'd done that himself before taking water himself. If it came down to him or his horse drinking, he'd give the water to his horse so the animal could keep carrying him.

She poured some water into her hat and let the horse drink it. Clint put his canteen back on his saddle and mounted.

"Already?" she asked, looking at him.

"If you can't keep up, you can—"

"I'll keep up," she said firmly. The horse finished the water and she put her canteen back on the saddle, put her hat on, and mounted. The hat tied beneath the chin with a thong, and she pushed the hat off her head so it rested behind her.

"Put the hat back on."

"Why? It's hot."

"That's why," he said. "You've got to keep your head covered or you'll get sunstroke."

She pulled the hat back up and secured it firmly on her head.

"If you really wanted me to turn back, you wouldn't have told me that," she said.

"I want you to turn back," he said, "but I don't want you dead."

"You know," she said, looking at him, "that might be the nicest thing you've said to me since we met."

"Let's get moving," he said with a growl.

Leave it to a woman to find a compliment where there wasn't one.

Chapter Twenty-Three

They came to a town called Staircase and stopped at the livery.

"We're looking for eight, maybe nine men," Clint said to the liveryman. "At least one of them will be driving a buckboard. The others will be mounted."

The liveryman, an elderly man with a gray growth of stubble beneath which his skin was shiny with sweat, rubbed his hand over his face. The sweat and dirt of his hand left streaks on his face.

"Ain't seen a buckboard," he said, "but they was four or five men on horseback."

"When was this?"

"Yesterday."

"Where did they go?"

"Ast me where the general store was."

"They didn't ask for a hotel?"

"No, just the general store and the saloon."

"All right, thank you," Clint said. "Would you look after our horses?"

"Sure. Staying overnight?"

Clint looked at Sara, who was exhausted, and then thought about the horses being pushed so hard in the intense heat.

"Yeah," he said finally, "yeah, overnight."

"Hotel's just down the street."

"Thanks."

Clint and Sara left the livery and Sara said, "You didn't have to do that, you know."

"Do what?"

"Decide to stay on my account."

"I didn't," he said. "The horses need the rest."

She accepted that without a word and trotted along next to him.

"Look," he said when they reached the hotel, "why don't you go into the hotel, get us a couple of rooms, and take a bath. I'll meet you over there in a little while."

"Where are you going?"

"The saloon, the general store."

"What for?" she asked. "The old man said he didn't see nine men, didn't see a buckboard."

"No, but he saw five men who wanted to know where to go to buy supplies," Clint said.

"And you think that those five—"

"I think maybe those five came into town for supplies while the others stayed camped somewhere outside the town, waiting. They didn't want to bring the gold into town. I can't say I blame them. Lots of dishonest people in the world."

"I can come with you—"

"Not to the saloon," Clint said.

"Now, wait—"

"You wait. A woman in a saloon attracts attention. I don't want to attract attention. You go to the hotel and get two rooms. You're paying."

"*I'm* paying—"

"Wells Fargo is paying, then," Clint said. "All I know is I'm not footing the bills."

"Clint—"

"Go take a bath, Sara," he said roughly and left her standing there.

Clint went to the saloon first and ordered a beer from the bartender, who was not yet thirty.

Clint paid for the beer, and when the bartender came back with his change he waved it away.

"What do I have to do for it?" the bartender asked suspiciously.

"Answer a couple of questions."

"Like what?"

"I'm interested in five men who came to town yesterday," Clint said. "Some or all of them would have come in here for a drink."

"There was a few strangers in here yesterday. They came in together."

"How many?"

"Maybe three."

The other two had probably gone to the general store for supplies.

"What did they talk about?"

"Oh, I don't know. I was busy—"

"Like you're busy now?" Clint asked. Besides himself there were only two other men in the saloon. There must have been another in town that was doing all the business. If the bartender here hadn't remembered the men, Clint would have to find the other saloon. He was pretty sure the men would have come here, though, to the smaller one, so as not to attract attention.

"I could maybe remember better—" the man started, but Clint reached over the bar and took hold of the man's collar, twisting it tight so it pressed on his Adam's apple.

"You'll remember, and I won't be squeezed for more money. Out of the goodness of my heart I'll still let you keep the change, but you better start talking to me real quick."

"Okay, okay," the man said, trying unsuccessfully to pull away from Clint's hold. "They were talking about taking a trip."

"To where?"

"Some foreign country."

Clint frowned.

"Mexico?"

"No," the man said, shaking his head. "I mean, I got the impression that they'd be in Mexico and that they'd start traveling from there."

"Describe them."

"What's to describe?" the bartender said with a shrug. "They all looked like saddle tramps, with worn guns and tired faces."

"What other impressions did you get?" Clint asked, releasing the man.

"Only that they were coming into a lot of money," he replied.

"How much is a lot?"

"I don't know," the bartender said, shrugging again. "I guess that depends on how much you have and how much you want, doesn't it?"

"It sure does," Clint said. He looked down at the change on the bar and then picked it up.

"Hey," the man said, plaintively, "you said I could keep that."

"I changed my mind," Clint said with a smile. "It's a lot of money."

Chapter Twenty-Four

Clint went to the general store next. Behind the counter was a handsome woman in her forties who remembered the two men he was talking about.

"What was it about them that was memorable?" he asked.

"Nothing physical, that's for sure. They were dirty with trail dust, and tired of traveling. They were very . . . complimentary to me, though."

"Complimentary."

"Yes, they . . . commented on my appearance," she said, touching her hair.

"What else did they say?"

"To me?"

She looked disappointed that he did not see fit to comment on her appearance, also.

"Or to each other."

"They were talking about someone named Bishop," she said, frowning as she tried to remember, "and that someone should teach him a lesson."

"Bishop?" Clint repeated. "Pete Bishop?"

"They didn't mention a second name, just Bishop."

"What kind of a lesson were they talking about?"

She smiled and said, "I don't know, but they didn't sound very happy with him."

"Is there anything else you can remember about them, Miss— "

"Mrs. Dodd," she said.

"Mrs. Dodd—anything else at all?"

"No, I'm afraid that's all," she said, "except that they were very . . . flattering."

"Yes, you mentioned that."

She was an attractive woman, but not as attractive as she thought she was. She was still waiting for him to toss a compliment her way.

She'd have a long wait.

"What was that name?" Sara asked.

She was fresh from a bath. Her hair was wet at the ends, and she smelled clean. She'd gotten them each a room, across the hall from one another, and they were talking in hers.

"Bishop," he said. "Pete Bishop."

"Who is he?"

"A gunman most of the time, a thief some of the time," Clint said.

"You know him?"

"I've heard of him."

"Does he know you?"

"He might have heard of me."

"Then maybe he sent those two men after you?"

"No."

"Why not? If he knows who you are—"

"A man like Pete Bishop would come after me himself," Clint said. "He wouldn't send a couple of incompetents to do the job for him."

"Why not?"

Clint frowned at her, knowing that he could try to explain it to her all day and she still wouldn't be able to understand.

"He just wouldn't."

"So what do we do now?"

"Go to Mexico."

"You think that's where they're going?"

"That's where I'd go if I'd just stolen a quarter of a million dollars in gold."

"Why?"

"No U.S. marshal could touch them there."

"But we could."

"I could."

"Are we going to have this argument again?"

"Sara—"

"I'm footing the bills, remember?"

She had a point there.

"Tell me something."

"What?"

"If we recover this gold, are we entitled to any reward?"

"Well, I'm not," she said. "I work for the company."

"So that means that I am?"

"Yes."

"How much?"

"Ten percent of what we recover."

Clint paused a moment to let that sink in.

"That means if we recover all of it, the reward would be . . . twenty-five thousand dollars?"

She did some quick mental figuring and said, "That's right."

"And you're paying me twenty-five hundred," he said. "You know, I could just go alone and pay all the bills myself."

"Ah, but I'd have to verify that you recovered the money," she said triumphantly. "I'd have to sign the paperwork before you got a cent."

He didn't know if she was telling the truth, but he

was impressed that she would try the ploy. The woman who came to his hotel that first day would never have thought of it.

"Okay," he said, "so we're going to Mexico."

Chapter Twenty-Five

They had supper that night in the hotel's small dining room, eating together in virtual silence. Clint simply had no desire to talk, and Sara couldn't think of a way to start a conversation.

Over coffee—Clint drinking it, and Sara watching him—Clint said, "You'd better turn in early tonight. I want to get an early start in the morning."

"Where are you going after dinner?"

"To buy some supplies and to pick up two fresh horses for us."

"Why fresh horses?"

"We're going to be pushing extra hard starting tomorrow."

"Harder than before?" she said before she could stop herself.

"Yeah," Clint said. "We're going to be taking a shortcut to Mexico."

"What kind of shortcut?"

"They're limited in where they can go because of the buckboard they're using to carry the gold," he explained. "We're not limited at all."

"I get the feeling we'd be better off getting some mules," she said.

"Let's just say we'll be off the beaten path a little," Clint said. "I also want to find the telegraph office—if they have one—and see what's going on in Caliente."

"I could do that," she said. "I also have to send a telegraph message to my company to let them know what's going on."

"All right," he said, "but after that you come back to the hotel."

"Why? I mean, why are you so insistent that I stay in the hotel?"

"Because it's possible they might have left someone behind to cover their trail," Clint said. "The best way for them to cover it would be to get you out of the way."

"Me?" she said. "Why me? Why not you?"

"Because you're paying me," Clint said. "Without you, they're home free."

"Wait a minute," she said, frowning. "Stop here for a minute."

"What is it?" he asked patiently. He lifted his coffee cup to his lips.

"Put the cup down!" she snapped.

Her vehemence surprised him. He didn't put the cup down, of course, but he *was* surprised. He took his sip and *then* put the cup down.

"What's wrong now?"

"Are you telling me that if I got killed tonight *you* would not continue chasing them?"

"Well, it's like you said, Sara," he said. "Without you I don't get the reward for retrieving the money. This may surprise you, but I don't usually do this sort of work if I don't get paid."

She stared at him for a few moments, speechless, and then said, "You really are a bastard, aren't you?"

"Not really," he said. "It's true I didn't know my parents, but I prefer to think that they were married when I was conceived." It was a lie, meant only as a smart reply.

"You sonofabitch!"

"Sara," he said, "you're really not the same girl I met in San Francisco."

"Thanks to you!" she said. "You're showing me the way people *should* live, aren't you? Just looking out for ourselves?"

"Don't be ridiculous," he said. "I'm not trying to tell you how to live. I live the way I see fit. If you learn from that, fine—"

"Learn?"

"—and if you don't, that's fine, too."

"You . . . you . . . you . . ." she said, half rising in her seat, as if standing would help her find the words she was looking for.

"You're still much too nice a girl to come up with the words you need at this moment," Clint said. "Why don't you just go and find the telegraph office and then go to your room." He stood up and said, "I'll take care of the bill here."

"Oh, no," she said, "I'm footing the bills, remember? I'll pay for dinner. You just go and do what you're going to do."

"All right," he said, choosing not to argue with her in her present state. "I'll see you in the morning."

"Sure," she said, not looking at him.

As he left she was waving at their waiter.

Actually, Clint doubted that the thieves would have left someone behind in this particular town. They probably would, however, once they got to Mexico, just to see who—if anyone— was following them there.

Clint wanted to get to Mexico ahead of them and be there waiting for them. He knew he was going to have to figure out some way to take care of nine men if he was going to recover the gold, but he was even more concerned with facing Pete Bishop.

Bishop did not have a big rep—not the way Hickok did—but he did have a fast gun. Clint was good at a lot of things. In fact, he was an excellent shot with a handgun or a rifle, but what he was *not* was a fast-draw artist. Whatever he did, however he decided to handle Pete Bishop, it sure as hell wouldn't be in a face-to-face confrontation on some street.

That'd be stacking his own deck against him.

No, if his plan worked and he got to Mexico ahead of Bishop and his men, he was going to have to have a definite plan on how to handle them.

The other thing on his mind as he walked to the general store was the man who had planned the robbery. Somebody with inside information had set this up, and Clint felt certain that man was *not* Pete Bishop. Bishop was the triggerman, and he was probably the man who had recruited the others, but the man *behind* the job was still to be identified, and would probably turn out to be one of Chief Stockton's men—if not the chief himself.

When he reached the general store he bought enough supplies to see them through a few days, but not enough to necessitate using a pack animal. That would negate the advantage they had as far as movement was concerned.

He arranged for the supplies to be delivered to the livery and then went there to buy two new animals. The liveryman wanted to haggle, but Clint was not one to waste time when he knew what he wanted to pay.

He made the liveryman see it his way and went back to the hotel.

When the knock came at his door, he knew it could only be Sara. Had she come to express her outrage again at his total lack of desire for revenge in the event she was killed? Clint had done very little in his life in the name of revenge, and he certainly wouldn't start now on a woman who was little more than a stranger to him. She couldn't understand that there was nothing he could—or wanted to—do about it.

He went to the door and opened it for her.

"I just wanted you to know I've had my company authorize you to act on their behalf in the event I'm killed," she said with great satisfaction. "That means you don't need me to earn that reward."

"That's very decent of you."

"How would you—" she started, intending to attack his use of the word "decent," but she stopped herself. "I also received a reply from Caliente. It seems Chief Stockton had taken some of his men and started after the thieves himself. They're probably not far behind us."

"If they're not," he said, "they soon will be. Anything else?"

"No, nothing else," she said stiffly. "I just wanted to see if you were taking your own advice."

"I'm turning in early and staying off the streets, just like I told you to do."

"And I'm going to do it right now," she said. "Good night."

"Good night, Sara."

Well, he thought after he'd closed the door, she's regained control of herself, he had to give her credit for that.

He went to the window and looked outside. In the morning he'd start moving at an entirely new pace. If she couldn't keep up, at least he wouldn't need her to authorize his reward.

He hadn't expected that from her.

Chapter Twenty-Six

Sara Denise Jones surprised Clint again the follow-ing day.

Most of their traveling that morning and afternoon had been off the roads, over rocky terrain, and she had stayed with him every step of the way. Although they had fresh horses, he couldn't give the horse all the credit. It was probably anger that kept her going—anger directed at him, and still as fresh as it was the day before.

When they camped that night she made no move to cook, so he told her to gather some wood chips for a fire. When they had the fire going he dumped a slab of bacon into a pan and a handful of coffee into the pot.

"You call that cooking?" she asked.

They were the first words she'd said to him since they'd stopped for a lunch of beef jerky.

"It's good enough," he said.

"What else did you buy besides beef jerky, bacon, and coffee?"

"Some canned peaches."

"That's all?"

"I wanted to travel light."

"Does that include getting rid of me?"

He didn't answer. He used his knife to cut the bacon up so it would cook faster.

Over dinner she said, "Doesn't it bother you?"

"What?"

"That I'm angry with you."

"No."

"You are the most . . . exasperating man."

"That may be . . ."

"It's not even worth being angry," she said. "It doesn't mean anything to you."

He remained silent.

"What *does* mean something to you, Clint?"

"Ten percent of a quarter of a million dollars."

"That's all?" she asked. "No friends?"

"One or two."

"No women?"

"A lot."

"No, I mean a special woman."

"No." Not the way she meant, anyway.

"Why are you answering all these personal questions all of a sudden?"

"That's a good question," he said. "Maybe because there's nothing else to do."

"I'm better than nothing, huh?"

"I wouldn't put it that way," he said. "If I was alone I'd probably still be traveling."

"At night?"

"A couple of more hours, at least," he said, "until it was really dark."

"So why not with me?"

"I don't need you getting thrown. That would really slow me down."

"You go to a lot of trouble to prove that I'm in the way, don't you?"

"No," he said. "I'm not proving anything. I'm just making conversation."

"Well, that's a start," she said.

"To what?"

"I don't know," she said. "I'll let you know when I figure it out."

When I figure you out, she added to herself.

She finished eating in silence. She'd decided not to ask him any more questions. All his answers did was confuse her more.

Clint fascinated her, and she didn't know how. Half the time she was repelled by him, the other half attracted to him. She didn't know which emotion was stronger, but whichever it was, the fascination was always there. She wanted to know why he said and did the things he did. What had happened to him—what, twenty years ago?— to turn him into the man he was today?

He'd never willingly tell her that, she knew that much. Even when he did answer her questions, they were short answers. He didn't give anything away.

She knew that what she should do was forget about him as a man and just see him as a means to get the gold back and safely delivered to Los Angeles.

The problem was that she hadn't been interested in a man in a long time.

Considering who she had become interested in now, maybe that was understandable.

Clint checked on the horses and then tossed some more wood chips and dried horse manure he'd collected along the way into the fire, to keep it going. It was a small fire, but at least it was a mild night and they didn't need it for warmth. It was just the right size for a pot of coffee, and he left one sitting there.

"Are you going to sleep?" Sara asked from the other side of the fire.

"In a while."

She propped herself up on her arm and asked, "You're not going to stand watch, are you?"

"No."

"Because if you are, I should—"

"Sara, if I was setting up a watch we'd split it, four on and four off."

"I'm sure we would," she said, lying back down on her blanket.

How could she have thought that he'd try to make it easier on her by standing watch without telling her?

"Go to sleep," he told her.

"That's what I intend to do," she said, turning her back to him.

Bastard!

Chapter Twenty-Seven

Their first stop in Mexico, five days after they left Caliente, was a small town called La Casa.

"Quaint name for a town," Sara said.

"Yeah."

They left the horses in the livery, registered in the La Casa hotel, and then went to have lunch in a small café the hotel clerk suggested.

"No steak," the waitress told Sara.

"Bueno," Clint told her. *"Dos enchiladas, y cerveza."*

"Con arroz?"

"Sí, por favor."

"What was all that about?"

"We're in Mexico, Sara," he said. "You don't order steak and potatoes."

"What do I order?" she asked. "What did *you* order?"

"Mexican food," he said. "Enchiladas and rice."

"And to drink?"

"Beer."

"What if I don't want beer?"

"Then don't drink it."

"I mean, it just so happens I do want beer, but you didn't even ask—"

"After what you ordered, I thought it would be better if I just went ahead."

"Oh, who cares?" she said. "As long as we eat. I'm so tired of bacon and canned peaches."

When the waitress brought the food she gave Sara a disapproving look, and Clint a smile filled with promise. She had dark skin and dark hair, a nose that was too big, and a full, voluptuous body that made men forget about her nose.

Clint didn't give her a second look.

"That waitress likes you," Sara said.

"Does she?"

"You didn't notice?"

"No. You'd better eat."

She tasted the food and obviously liked it because she continued eating without speaking until she was done.

When the waitress returned Clint told her, *"Café."*

"Sí, señor."

"I don't need a translation to know what you ordered this time."

"Coffee."

"I know," she said, annoyed. "I said I didn't need a translation."

"So you did."

"Look, Clint, how do we know where they're going to come into Mexico?"

"Mexicali, most likely, and then on through toward Santa Ana."

"Why that way?"

"They'll want to get as far south as they can get before they stop and divvy up the gold. That's the most direct route. Don't forget, they've got to stick to the main road with that wagon."

"So where will we wait? Here?"

"Santa Ana, I think," Clint said. "It's a bigger town than this, though not by any means a big town. It'll do, though."

"When will we get there?"

"Tomorrow, late afternoon sometime."

"Are we spending the night here?"

"Yes."

"Do you think there's a telegraph office in town?"

"I didn't see any wires when we rode in."

She had something on her mind, but he'd listen when she figured out how to bring it out. He wasn't going to sit there and yank it out of her.

The coffee came, and this time Clint looked at the waitress. She smiled at him and he nodded to her, but he wasn't interested in her for any reason but that she had brought his coffee.

Also—rather pointedly, in fact—she brought one cup and placed it very carefully in front of Clint, then looked at Sara to see how she'd take it.

Sara smiled and said, "Thanks, but I don't care for any right now."

The waitress frowned—probably because she hadn't succeeded in insulting Sara—and walked away.

"She's going to be very disappointed if you don't come back later."

"Let her." He poured himself a cup of coffee and then looked at Sara. "I'm going to be a while drinking this. Why don't you go for a walk, or go back to the hotel."

"Am I bothering you?"

"Hell, no, you're not bothering me."

"Are you concerned for my feelings?"

He put his cup down and stared at her.

"I am not an uncaring man, Sara, but I am getting tired of you trying to trap me into admitting to some . . . some emotion that you'd like to see me exhibit just so you can pinpoint your opinion of me."

She was taken aback by his statement because that was exactly what she'd been trying to do, pinpoint her opinion of him.

He drank his first cup of coffee in silence, and by the time he poured his second she seemed to have worked out what she wanted to say.

"You've done this before, haven't you?"

"Done what?"

"Hunted men."

"Yes, I've done it before."

"How long does it usually take?"

He smiled. It might have been the first real smile she'd seen from him.

"Sara, there's no way I can answer that question."

"Well, what was the longest it ever took you to hunt a man down?"

"One man? Two years."

"No, I meant—wait, did you say . . . two years?"

"Yes."

"To hunt down one man?"

"Yes."

"Well . . . what did he do that would make you spend two years hunting him?"

Clint stared at her.

"That's not a question I'd like to answer right now."

"But—"

"Sara, go on with what you were saying," Clint said, cutting her off.

"Can we talk about this another time?" she asked.

"Ask me another time."

She looked at him for a few moments, then nodded to herself.

"All right," she said. "What's the quickest you ever hunted a man and found him?"

"A few hours—again, we're talking about one man."

"It'll take longer for nine, huh?"

"That depends on what you want."

"What do you mean?"

"Do you want the nine men brought in, or will you be satisfied with the gold? If we find one man, and he has the gold, do we forget about the other eight?"

"Wells Fargo is only concerned with the gold."

"Then again," he said, "we might find the gold and all nine men at the same time. Then we'll have no choice in the matter."

"Are you talking about killing again?"

"Sara, you don't think those nine men are just going to hand that gold over to us, do you?"

"Then . . . how will we get it?"

"I've been thinking about that myself."

"And?"

"And I haven't come up with a plan yet."

"But you will?"

"Of course I will," he answered. "That's what you're paying me for, isn't it?"

She gave him a frown and said, "Now you're humoring me."

"Sara, all I can tell you is that I'll try my best to get that gold back."

"I guess I can't ask for any more than that, huh?"

"Someone else might be able to give you more than my best," he said, "but my best is all *I* have to offer."

"I think I'd settle for your best," she said, "above anyone else's."

"Is that so?" he said. "Why don't you reserve your decision until you've *seen* my best?"

She stood up and said, "I think I'll go for a walk. I'll see you at the hotel."

"Sure."

She left the café and he poured himself a third cup of coffee. Seeing Sara leave, the waitress hurried over to see if there was anything else she could do for him.

Anything at all.

Chapter Twenty-Eight

Clint left the café without making any promises to the waitress. He did not, however, reject her. She did, after all, have a very nice body.

He made a slow circuit of the town, which didn't take very long. La Casa was simply a collection of run-down adobe buildings and some falling-down wooden shacks.

Clint found the *cantina* in one of the adobe buildings and went inside for a beer. There were four other men in the place, two sitting together, one sitting alone, and the other standing at the bar. The one sitting alone was American, while the other three were Mexicans.

Clint accepted his beer from the bartender and studied the seated man in the mirror behind the bar. Was he one of the gold thieves, sent ahead to scout around? Or had they beaten him and Sara to Mexico, and this man had been left behind?

Or was he not connected with them at all?

Clint called the bartender over.

"Do you speak English?"

"Sí, señor."

Clint put some money on the bar.

"*Señor,* you have already paid for the *cerveza.*"

"This is not for the beer," Clint said.

"Then . . . for what?"

"A question."

The man shrugged and waited for the question.

"The gringo sitting at the table behind me."

"I see him."

"How long has be been here?"

The man shrugged again and said, "About two hours—"

"No, I mean here in town."

"Oh." The bartender rubbed his dark-stubbled jaw and then said, "About a week, I think."

"Could it be less?"

"Maybe a day or two, but no more."

Clint pushed the money across the bar to the man, who took it.

"Is that all?"

"That's all. Thanks."

"*Por nada, señor.*"

The bartender went away and Clint looked again at the man at the table. If the bartender was right and he had been here five to seven days, then he couldn't be one of the thieves.

During his walk around town Clint had not seen another gringo. As far as he was concerned, the gold thieves had not passed through here. He was still sure that Santa Ana was the place where they'd cross paths.

He started back to the hotel and then hesitated right there in the street. If he went to the hotel he might end up on the butt end of more questions from Sara. She might even ask *that* question again.

When he had answered her question, he had done so without thinking. Two years, he'd told her. It wasn't until after he'd replied that he realized what he'd said.

He didn't want to think about the answer to that question.

He turned and walked away from the hotel, toward the café again, and the waitress with the big nose and the even bigger breasts.

Chapter Twenty-Nine

When Clint woke the next morning the waitress was nestled between his legs. She was nuzzling him, her big nose buried in his pubic hair, her educated tongue bringing him fully awake. When she took him into her mouth he reached down and cupped her head in both hands and, finding her tempo, matched it with his hips. . . .

They were in her room above the café. He'd been surprised to find that she not only worked in the café, but also owned it. Further, he'd found out that she was perfectly happy living in La Casa and had no desire to get married and leave.

Her name was Estralita, and she'd been very pleased when he'd returned the previous evening. She had closed the café immediately and, taking him by the hand, led him upstairs to her bed.

There was very little conversation between them because she did not speak English, and his Spanish was limited to being able to order food and drink. Still, there was little reason for conversation between them. Both knew what they wanted from the other, and both gave it freely and—at times—eagerly.

Clint had spent a long time on her voluptuous breasts the night before. They were not only larger but also very firm, and her flesh was as smooth as glass. He couldn't get enough of licking her tits and sucking her nipples, and she certainly didn't complain about the excess attention. She, in fact, gave his cock the same sort of attention, so they came out pretty even as far as who was giving who more pleasure. . . .

Now Clint flipped her over onto her belly, and she eagerly got onto her elbows and knees and raised her butt for him. He straddled her and plunged into her, taking her very forcefully. She buried her face in her pillow and cried out as he spurted into her. . . .

Later she watched him as he dressed to leave. They had both gotten what they wanted from each other, and there were no regrets.

"*Adiós,*" he said.

"*Vaya con Dios,*" she said with a smile.

Clint found Sara at the livery.

"I knocked on your door this morning but there was no answer," she said.

"Maybe that's because I wasn't there."

She stared at him for a moment, then said, "Oh."

Disappointment was plain on her face. What the hell did she have to be disappointed about?

"Are you ready to ride?" he asked her.

"Sure," she said. "I'm well rested. *I* got enough rest last night."

He decided to let the remark go. He'd already spent more time with her than he had spent with a woman in a long time. She was starting to sound like a wife.

"How long to Santa Ana?" she asked, mounting up and sidling over next to him.

"Six hours hard riding," he said. "We can make it in eight. There's no hurry."

"How can you be sure?"

"I'm not *sure*," he said. "Not absolutely. It's just the way I feel. There's no need to punish the horses if we don't have to."

"And when we reach Santa Ana?"

"When we get there we'll wait."

"How long?"

"However long it takes."

"For what?"

"For them to get there, or for me to decide that I've made a mistake."

"Oh, you make mistakes?" She said it as if it were news to her.

"I make a hell of a lot of mistakes," he said, "and unlike most people, I admit when I've made them—like taking this job."

"What are you so testy about this morning?"

He glared at her and did not answer. He *was* testy, and even he wasn't sure why, so how could he answer her?

"Let's get started," he said.

"I thought there was no hurry?"

"There isn't—unless we sit here and talk all blasted morning!"

Chapter Thirty

Pete Bishop had decided that if and when the time came when he would need to count on somebody, he had only two choices.

Jack Pine was a fair hand with a gun, and a good man to have to your side in a fight. He was not as openly eager to see the gold as the others, and didn't seem to mind doing what he was told.

Sam Forester was a smart man. He clearly understood that Pete Bishop could kill any two of them and take a third man with him on his way down if they chose to try to take the gold from him. There were not three men who were willing to die for the chance, least of all Forester. He was also a fair hand with a gun, but he wasn't as big as Pine, so Bishop didn't know how well he'd fare in a fistfight.

It was Pine and Forester to whom Pete Bishop would look if he found he needed help.

They had passed through Mexicali, and Bishop had told them that the next town they would stop in would be Santa Ana.

"When do we get to look at the gold?" Cal Benedict asked.

If the rest of them were going to choose a new leader among themselves, Bishop felt it would be Benedict.

"When we meet Teddy in Santa Ana."

"Well, he'd better be there waiting for us," Benedict said.

"He won't be," Bishop assured him. "He probably didn't leave Caliente for two days after we did."

"Two days?" Benedict said. "You mean even after we get to Santa Ana we got to wait two days for our share? That don't seem fair."

Some of the other men spoke up about the unfairness of it, in agreement with Benedict.

"Nobody said anything about being fair," Bishop said. "While you're riding with me, you'll do as I say, fair or no. Is that clear?"

"It's clear, Pete," Jack Pine said, and Bishop saw Sam Forester nod his agreement. A couple of the other men agreed as well.

"Ain't there any towns between here and Santa Ana?" Benedict asked. He wasn't quite ready to give it up.

"There are," Bishop said.

"Then why don't we stop at one of them?"

"Because that's not the plan."

"I'm getting awful tired of hearing about this plan—" Benedict complained.

"You didn't argue with the plan when it went perfectly at the train," Pete Bishop reminded him, cutting him off. "If you disagree with it now, Cal, feel free to ride out on your own."

All of the other men focused on Cal Benedict now, and if he was going to make a stand, that would have been the time.

"I ain't about to ride out without my share, Bishop," he finally said.

"Then shut up for a while. We've got a long ride ahead of us, and I ain't about to make it with you jawing at me the whole way."

Benedict glared at Bishop's back as the man rode on ahead of him. He gave shooting the man in the back one brief thought, then decided against it.

The time will come, he told himself, and when it does, I won't have to move alone.

Chapter Thirty-One

Santa Ana was considerably larger than any town Clint and Sara had encountered since entering Mexico.

"At last," Sara said as they entered the town, "a real town, with a decent hotel and a telegraph office. I'm going to take a long soak in a hot tub."

"You do that."

During the entire ride Clint had been quiet, and when he wasn't quiet he was surly, as he was now. Maybe, she thought, this is the real Clint. At least if it was, she wouldn't have to worry about being attracted to him anymore.

Somehow, though, she didn't think that was going to be the case.

She was sure it had been a question she'd asked him, but for the life of her she couldn't recall when it might have been.

Maybe it wasn't that at all. Maybe it wasn't even something she'd done. Maybe it was that waitress he'd dallied with in La Casa.

She hoped he'd caught some sort of an itch from her!

After leaving the horses at the livery, they went to the hotel and registered.

"Do you have bath facilities?" Clint asked.

"Oh *sí señor*," the well-dressed clerk said. "The very best in all of Mexico." He pronounced it "Me-hi-co."

"The lady will have a bath," Clint said. "A hot one."

"Of course," the man said, giving Sara an approving look. "And for the *senor*?"

"Maybe later," Clint said.

"Would ten minutes be soon enough for you?" the clerk asked Sara.

"Yes, fine. Thank you."

They turned and moved toward the stairs.

"Here, take my key," Clint said. "Put my saddlebags in my room before you take your bath."

"Where are you going?"

"I want to take a quick look around town," Clint said. "When I come back I'll have a bath. If you want to get something to eat, go—"

"I'll wait for you," she said. "You're the one who knows how to order in Spanish."

"All right," he said, handing her his saddlebags. "I'll be back in a little while."

Sara went upstairs and Clint went out the front door to the street.

It took longer to make a circuit of this town than it did La Casa, and there were a lot more white faces this time. It wasn't going to be so easy to eliminate them one by one.

Clint went back to the livery and made an excuse for wanting to look at his horse. Once inside the stable he checked around for horses that looked as if they'd ridden in not too long ago. There were a couple, but there weren't nine or ten. He checked out the back door for a buckboard. There was a buggy but no buckboard. The buggy could not have been used to transport gold.

From the livery he located the telegraph office. He didn't use it just then, but he wanted to know where it was for when he did want to use it.

After that he stopped at the saloon for a beer, and then went back to the hotel.

"My key," he said to the clerk.

"¿Señor?"

"Did my friend leave my key here?"

"Oh, the señora? She is in the bath."

"Still?" Clint said.

"The ladies, they like to—how do you say—soak?"

"Yeah, soak. Did she leave my key?"

"Oh," the clerk said. He turned and checked the box for Clint's room. "Sí señor," the clerk said, handing him his key. "You room number is seis—uh, six."

"And the señora?"

"Ah, yes, your amiga," the man said with a wide grin. "She is in room siete—uh, seven."

"Thank you."

"Por nada."

Clint went upstairs and entered his room. His saddlebags were on the bed. Sara was still using the bath, so he sat back on the bed to wait his turn.

He still hadn't a clue as to how he was going to take a quarter of a million dollars in gold away from nine men who sure wouldn't want to part with it.

He also wondered if Bishop and his men were just going to ride into town with the gold bold as brass.

He got up and went to the window. He could just see them riding straight down the main street, eight men on horseback and one man driving a buckboard that was hauling heavy.

Who'd notice them, right?

Now, if one lone man drove a buckboard into town, nobody would look at him twice. Hell, in a town like this eight men riding in together might not even attract attention. Some people might even figure they were on the run from Texas, New Mexico, or California, and who'd care if they were? This was Mexico, not the United States.

Clint wondered what the local *jefe* was like. How would he feel about a gang of American desperadoes riding into his town?

Clint didn't think he'd get any help there. Most of the local sheriffs were as sleepy as their towns. They generally gave American fugitives and Mexican *bandidos* anything they wanted just to keep the town safe.

No, there'd be no help there. Clint was going to have to work this one on his own, with whatever assistance Sara could offer— and he hadn't known her long enough to figure out just how much help she would be.

That was something he was going to have to find out when the time came.

Sara's room was right next to his, and he heard her enter. He left his room and knocked on her door. When she opened it he stared at her for a moment. She still had a towel in her hand and was drying her hair, which she had washed. She had a well-scrubbed look and a clean smell, and he realized in that moment that she *was* a very attractive woman.

"Finished your bath, I see."

"It was wonderful," she said, "even if the tub is a little small. You're going to have a hell of a time getting in and out of it."

"I'll do the best I can," he said. "I'll see you after my bath and we'll go and have some dinner."

"You'll have to tell me your plan," she said as he started to walk away.

"Plan?"

"For getting the gold back."

"Oh, yes," he said, "that plan."

"You do have a plan, don't you?"

"Of course I have a plan," he said. "I wouldn't be very good at what I do if I didn't have a plan, would I?"

"That's funny," she said. "That's the first hint of humor I've seen in you since we met."

"Is it?"

"And it means we're in trouble."

"Does it?"

"You don't have a plan, do you?"

"Don't I?" Clint said, and walked off down the hall.

"No," she said to his retreating back, "you don't."

Chapter Thirty-Two

After dinner they walked around the town together.

"If you're going to have some kind of a confrontation in a strange town," he explained, "the best thing for you to do is familiarize yourself with it as much as you can."

"I understand."

She was a very good listener, very attentive as he explained the ins and outs of preparing for trouble.

"Do you have your gun on you?" he asked.

"It's in my bag."

"First chance you get," he said, "take it out and tuck it down into your belt. It should be where you can get at it in a hurry."

"I'm anything but a fast draw, Clint," she said wryly.

"That doesn't matter, Sara. The point is to get the gun out quickly, but not to fire a shot until you're sure you can hit something. A lot of these fast-draw artists can get the gun out in the wink of an eye, but they don't know what to do with it once it's out."

She stared at his face, nodding as the truth of what he was telling her penetrated.

"Most shots fired in haste are clean misses, Sara. The deliberate shot is the truest."

"I understand."

Clint wished he had time to see how well she could shoot, but any kind of target practice near town would attract attention. If he took her away from the town, they might miss any arrival of their prey.

"What do we do now?" she asked as they headed back to the hotel.

"One of us has to be watching the streets at all times," Clint said. "We've got to know as soon as they arrive."

"*If* they arrive."

"Yes, Sara," he said, "*if* they arrive. That's the sensible way to look at it."

"And if they don't arrive?"

"Why don't we wait a few days," Clint said. "We couldn't be more than that far ahead of them with the shortcuts we took. If they don't arrive by then, we'll go on to the next step."

"Wait a minute," she said, putting her hand on his arm as he turned to go into the hotel.

"What is it?"

"You're not getting away that easy."

"Away from what?"

"Don't play coy, Clint," she said. "You promised to tell me your plan."

"I didn't make any promises, Sara," he said. "I never do."

"Why not?"

"Because then I won't be forced to break them."

"Is that what you think promises are for?"

"That's what I think usually happens with a promise," he said.

"Anyway, you claimed to have a plan."

"And you called me a liar."

"So tell me, then," she said. "What's your plan?"

"I can't tell you right here."

"Then come on," she said, grabbing his hand.

"Where are we going?"

"Back to the café," she said. "I'm going to buy you a pot of coffee. In fact, I may even have a cup."

"You want to know this plan very badly," he said, "don't you?"

They went to the same café where they had just eaten. Clint sat with his back to the wall, so he could look right out the front window at the main street.

"All right, all right," she said eagerly, "what's the plan?"

"Guile," he said over his cup.

"What?"

"We'll take the gold from them through guile."

"You mean . . . trick them out of it?"

"Yes."

"Will we have time to do that?" she asked. "I mean, won't they . . . divvy it up as soon as they arrive?"

"No, I think they'll wait for the brains to arrive," Clint said, "if for no other reason than he is probably the only one who can divide."

"That still doesn't give us much time."

"Two days."

She looked at him with an exasperated expression on her face.

"How do you make these judgments?"

"Experience," he said simply.

"All right," she said. "Why do you think that the brains behind this theft won't arrive for two days?"

"Because he'll want to wait until some of his henchmen kill each other."

"What?"

He put his cup down.

"He knows that many men around that much gold, just sitting around waiting for him, will lead to trouble. What we're going to do is make sure he's right."

"Add fuel to the fire, you mean?"

"That's right," he said. Suddenly he was studying her in a different way.

"What's the matter?" she asked.

She had no way of knowing it, but Clint had just come up with his plan.

"How do you look in a peasant blouse?"

Chapter Thirty-Three

Clint sat on a chair in front of the hotel the following morning while Sara went shopping.

She had not been immediately receptive to the part she would play in his plan, but finally agreed to go and do the shopping.

"Not that there's going to be much to choose from in this town," she said.

"Just pick up whatever you can that looks like a peasant blouse," he said. "You know, something that comes real low—"

"I know what you want, Clint," Sara said, "and I'll try and give it to you—but I won't like it."

"How do you know?"

"Trust me. . . ."

Now he watched the town go by and was struck at how slow everyone in Santa Ana moved. It was as if the town were existing in slow motion.

He was sitting comfortably, with the chair tipped back on its rear legs and his feet up on the wooden rail in front of him, when the sheriff came over.

"Señor," the man said, inclining his head.

"Sheriff."

"You are newly arrived in Santa Ana, are you not?"

the man asked. He was tall and slender, with a well-cared-for mustache and a red sash around his waist. Tucked into the sash was a long-barreled Colt. Except for the kind of gun, the guy thought he was the reincarnation of Wild Bill Hickok.

"Yes, I am."

"Passing through?"

"Well, I thought I might stay for a few days, just take it easy, you know?"

"*Sí, señor,*" the sheriff said, "I know exactly what you mean."

Clint thought the man might go away after that, but instead the lawman put his foot up on the boardwalk and leaned on his knee, regarding Clint amiably.

"So tell me, *señor,*" he said, "what did you do?"

"What did I do?"

"*Sí.*"

"What did I do to who?"

"Oh, please, *señor,*" the sheriff said, "a man such as yourself does not come to Santa Ana unless he is—on the run, as you say."

"I don't say," Clint said, "you say, Sheriff. I'm not on the run."

"Very well, *señor,*" the sheriff said, "you may keep your . . . problems to yourself, but I would not like it if you created new problems in my town."

"New problems?"

"I would not want you to . . . uh, break the law here."

"I have no intentions of breaking the law."

"That is good," the sheriff said, taking his foot off the boardwalk. "*Señor,* I am afraid I must ask you for your name."

"It's Clint Adams."

If the sheriff recognized the name, he didn't let it show on his face.

"And the lady, *señor*," the sheriff said, "she is your woman?"

"She is . . ." Clint said, starting to say that she was *not*, but then he thought better of it and stopped. "She is my lady."

"And her name?"

"Sara Jones."

"Jones," the man said, nodding. "It is amazing, *señor*, how many americanos we get in Santa Ana named Smith and Jones."

"And Brown?"

"*Sí*, and Brown."

"I'm sure it is."

"*Señor*," he said, standing at attention, "I am Carlos Hernando Armando Colón DeLeon, *el jefe* of Santa Ana, and I must warn you that my eye will be on you during your stay here."

"I find that very comforting, Sheriff."

"You do?"

Clint nodded.

"*Very* comforting."

The man looked puzzled for a moment, then said, "Good day, *señor*," and walked away.

"Good day, Sheriff DeLeon."

As the lawman looked away, Clint shook his head at his fortune—or misfortune—to have found the only overzealous sheriff in all of Mexico.

When Sara finished her shopping, she found Clint sitting in front of the hotel.

"Taking it easy?" she asked.

"I've just been thoroughly grilled by the local law," he told her, "and I'm exhausted."

"What did he want?"

"He wanted me to know that he would have his eye

on us while we were here."

"Why?"

"Because he's under the impression that we did something."

"Did what?"

"Something that has us on the run from the United States."

"That's absurd," she said. "I'll go and show him my credentials—"

"Never mind your credentials," Clint said. "Let's go upstairs so you can show me what you have in those packages."

"These packages?"

"Those packages, right under your arm," he said, pointing. "Were you able to find something like I described?"

"Actually, I was surprised at what I found."

"Well," Clint said, standing up, "let's go upstairs and you can surprise *me*."

Clint suggested that she change in his room, so he could stay by the window and watch the street.

"You'd like that, wouldn't you?" she said. "I'll change in my room and then come to your room."

"Suit yourself," he said. "I assure you my interest is not in catching a glimpse of your lily-white body."

"Nevertheless . . ." she said, and went to her own room.

Clint went into his room to wait and kept an eye on the street. He heard it before he saw it. A buckboard has a distinctive sound, especially since so few of them are well made. It also helped that, even though Santa Ana was larger than other towns they'd passed through, it was no less sleepy and quiet.

He watched as the buckboard, drawn by two horses, made its way down the main street toward the livery.

There was one man driving it, and on the back there was something covered by a tarp.

Behind him he heard his door open.

"Clint—" Sara said.

"Looks like we hit paydirt, Sara," he said.

"Really?"

He felt her move behind him, pressing lightly against him.

"The buckboard?" she asked in his ear.

"The buckboard."

She was wearing perfume, and had used a little too much of it. She leaned more heavily on him, and he felt unfettered breasts flattening against his back. Unfettered, that is, beneath her clothes.

"Any sign of the other men?" she asked.

"No, not yet," he said. "They'll probably ride in later in the day."

The pressure on his back stopped as she moved away from the window.

"Well," he started to say, "let's have a look—" As he turned to examine her in her new clothes, he was brought up short by what he saw.

"I, uh, thought it would have a better effect if I, uh, did something with my . . . my hair?"

She had done something with her hair, which up until now had been worn in some kind of a bun behind her head. Now it was down around her shoulders, soft and light. She was wearing a peasant blouse that showed her round breasts to their best advantage, and a skirt that revealed sound calves.

She looked like an entirely different Sara Denise Jones.

"You're staring," she said self-consciously.

She waited for a comment from him, and when one was not forthcoming she said, "I bought a couple of other blouses, just in case this one wasn't what you had in mind."

"Uh, no, no," he said, finding his voice. "This is fine. This one is exactly what I did have in mind."

"Well . . . good," she said.

"Give me a turn or two."

She did a slow pirouette for him, and then a quicker one. Her skirt swirled and showed him that her thighs were as firm and smooth as her calves.

"Very becoming."

"That's the first compliment you've ever given me," she said.

"I wasn't under the impression that you hired me to supply compliments."

"No, you're right. I didn't," she said. "Then you think this will do the trick?"

"I think this will do very nicely," he said. "Very nicely, indeed."

Chapter Thirty-Four

The other men arrived in three different groups during the course of the day, and by dark they were all present.

The last group to ride into town was comprised of three men, and Clint recognized Pete Bishop from the descriptions he had heard of him.

"Is that him?" Sara asked.

"That's him, in the center," Clint said.

They were watching from Clint's window as the last three men rode in. Sara had changed back into her own clothes, but she had left her hair down, and she still smelled of that perfume.

"Tell me again what you want me to do."

"I want you to catch their attention," Clint said. "Play up to them."

"All of them?"

"Pick three or four," he said.

"And?"

"And what?"

They both straightened and moved away from the window.

"And play up to them."

"To what extent?"

He knew what she was asking. How far did he want her to go?

"Just . . . make enough promises to them to get them thinking."

"And?"

"And enough to get them mad at each other."

"And what am I to do with these promises?"

"What are promises made for?"

"To be broken?"

"Exactly."

"That's your philosophy, not mine . . ." she said.

"But under these circumstances . . ." he said.

"Yes . . . I suppose so."

"Just dress the way you were dressed before and be . . . coquettish."

"Coquettish."

"Yes . . . flirtatious."

"I know what coquettish means, Clint," Sara said. "I'm just not sure I can . . . be flirtatious."

"The way you look . . . looked before, you'll do just fine."

"You . . . you liked the way I looked before?"

"You looked . . . just fine, Sara," Clint said. "You'll do just fine."

"Just fine, huh?"

"Sara—"

"Should we start this little charade tomorrow?" she asked, cutting him off.

"No," Clint said, "I think we'd better start it off tonight."

"Tonight?"

"Sure. Some of them will have to be at the *cantina* tonight."

"What do you want me to do?"

"I just want you to walk in," he said, "and walk out.

Give them a good look at you."

She took a deep breath and said, "Well, damn it, all right."

"And at the same time," he said, as she went to the door, "you can take a look at them, see which three or four you want to play up to."

"From what I've seen so far," she said, "I don't think there's much to choose from."

She opened the door and he said, "One more thing, before you get dressed."

"What's that?"

"Don't play up to Pete Bishop."

"Jealous already?"

"No," he said, "he just won't take the bait. He's not the type to look at a skirt and let it distract him from his job."

"You mean . . . like you?"

Chapter Thirty-Five

When Clint entered the *cantina* he knew that there was a slight chance that Pete Bishop might recognize him, but he decided to play the odds. He was pretty well known in San Francisco and Sacramento, but maybe his "fame," such as it was, had not yet spread to other regions. And as far as he knew, Bishop had never been to San Francisco. He plied his trade mostly in Texas, Arizona, and New Mexico.

He walked into the *cantina* and saw that more than half of the new arrivals were there. Bishop was among the men who were missing.

They had taken two tables, and were drinking and whooping it up. Apparently they weren't as shy about drinking together as they were about riding into town together.

Clint walked to the bar and ordered a beer. Sara would be entering in about ten minutes. He contrived to blend in with the surroundings until that time.

He watched the celebration through the mirror behind the saloon and saw that there was one girl working the *cantina*. She was about twenty-five, with dark hair and a slender but taut figure. She was wearing a peasant blouse not unlike the one Sara would be wearing, but her breasts were smaller than Sara's and certainly not

145

as round. Still, there were hard little points pushing out against the fabric, and most of the men were eyeing her appreciatively. Clint was certain that, as attractive as this girl was, there would have to be two or three of the men who would prefer Sara.

Wouldn't there?

Pete Bishop had decided long before their arrival in Santa Ana that he would not be joining the celebrations of his men. He knew that most of them were at the saloon, while a few of them had immediately sought out the town whorehouse. Bishop was in his hotel room, looking out his window at the main street. As he watched a well-built American woman in a peasant blouse cross the street, he wondered if Teddy would be arriving on time. He was supposed to be no more than two days behind them, but if something had gone wrong, would Bishop be able to keep the men from the gold for longer than that?

The buckboard and the gold were in the livery with one man— at this time Jack Pine—guarding it. He would be relieved by Sam Forester, who would in turn be relieved by Bishop himself.

They were supposed to be guarding the gold from prying eyes and not from their own "colleagues," but Bishop had made it clear to both men that no one was to go near the gold—*no one*. Both Pine and Forester knew they'd have to tangle with Bishop if anything went wrong.

Bishop was still watching the woman, who seemed to be heading for the saloon. He assumed from the way she was dressed that she worked there.

Bishop would save his womanizing until the gold was divvied up. He'd been afraid that all he was going to have to pick from were dark-haired Mexican women. It looked like that wouldn't be the case.

He decided it wouldn't hurt to go down to the saloon to take a look at her now.

Sara Jones paused outside the *cantina* and dried her sweaty palms on the side of her skirt. She looked down at her bosom and wondered if her breasts would fall out if she bent over. She didn't know how women wore these things all the time.

She'd examined herself critically in the mirror in her hotel room, and she had to admit that she didn't look bad. If she was any judge, she figured that Clint thought she looked all right, too. He hadn't been staring at her for nothing. When he saw her breasts his eyes had just about bugged out of his head.

Maybe there was a chance, after all this was finished . . .

And if Clint was still alive . . .

She adjusted herself and walked into the *cantina*.

As soon as Sara walked in, Clint saw some of the men notice her. They nudged the men who hadn't, and pretty soon all eyes were on her as she walked to the bar. She remembered what he'd told her, and stood with plenty of space between her and Clint.

"Beer," she said.

"*¿Señorita?*" the bartender said, frowning.

"You do serve ladies, don't you?"

"*No comprende, señorita,*" the bartender said.

Clint knew the man was lying. He'd heard him speak English— heavily accented, but English nevertheless. He spoke it and understood it. He just didn't want to serve her.

Clint watched the men through the mirror, and one of them got up and approached the bar.

"Can I help you, ma'am?" he asked.

He was in his late twenties, and even Clint had to admit he was a good-looking cuss. Smooth-faced and lean, with not an ounce of fat on him.

"Well, I would like a beer if I could get this gentleman to serve me."

The man's back was to Clint, but he'd have bet a lot that he was looking down the front of her blouse, where her breasts swelled.

The man turned to the bartender and ordered a beer in rapid-fire Spanish. When the bartender brought it, he presented it to Sara with a flourish.

"You're very kind," she said. The way she was looking at him even Clint would have thought she was taken with him, if he didn't know any better.

And she wasn't sure she could pull it off.

From what he could see, Sara Jones was a natural-born flirt.

Damn her.

Chapter Thirty-Six

Clint kept his place at the end of the bar and watched as, one by one, the other men moved to try their brand of charm on Sara.

The Mexican gal who was working the room didn't look happy. She was glaring at Sara, and if looks could kill, Sara would have been dead ten times already.

Then the Mexican girl noticed Clint, who was still standing at the end of the bar, and moved to his side.

"You do not like *gringo* women, *señor*?"

"If wanted *gringo* women I'd go back to Texas," he told her. "They're too pale. I like women with dark hair and smooth, dark skin, like yours."

"I am happy to hear that, *señor*," she said. She pressed against him so that the tips of her pert breasts were mashed against him. He felt her hard nipples digging into him.

Clint figured that to look less conspicuous he'd better play like the Mexican women appealed to him, while the other men were fussing over Sara.

He had slid his arm around the Spanish girl's little waist when the batwing doors opened and Pete Bishop stepped into the saloon.

For a moment Clint thought that Bishop was looking right at him, but then the man's eyes passed him and continued on. Two of his men were still seated, but four of them were clustered around Sara, who looked to Clint to be enjoying the attention.

"Boys," Bishop said to the two seated men. He walked over to their table, and Clint was able to hear the conversation.

"What's going on?"

"The boys have found themselves a woman, boss," one man said.

"There are plenty of women in town," Bishop said.

"Not like this one," the other man said.

"What's so special about this one?"

"She's white, not Mexican."

Bishop's head turned, and he studied the group at the bar. For a moment he looked undecided about whether to sit or walk over, but he finally moved toward the bar.

"Beer," he told the bartender.

"Hey, hi, boss," one of the men said, noticing him.

"Hello, Jess. Who's the lady?"

Bishop's men moved back so he could see Sara, and Bishop moved closer to her.

The girl at Clint's side began to fidget, but Clint wanted to hear what Bishop had to say to Sara.

"*¿Señor?*" she said, rubbing up against him like a cat. "I have a room upstairs."

Clint was about to answer her when he saw the two men who were still seated studying him. They knew what the girl wanted, and if Clint didn't go with her they'd get suspicious of him.

Clint had warned Sara that he might not be able to stay with her the whole time. She understood that.

"What's your name?" he asked the girl.

"Rosa."

"All right, Rosa," he said, "let's go up and take a look at that room."

Rosa took Clint's hand and tugged him toward the steps. Sara was deep in conversation with Bishop while the other men milled about, and she never gave Clint a second glance.

Apparently she was in complete control.

When they entered the room, Rosa wasted no time. She pulled the blouse down her arms so that her pert, brown-tipped breasts popped free. Her nipples were hard, and she was biting her bottom lip.

"I want it bad, mister," she said, as if she were warning him.

"My name is Clint," he said, but she was beyond hearing him. She pulled off her skirt, showing him her slim hips, strong thighs, and black pubic patch. Her eyes had a glazed look to them, and her lips looked swollen.

This little filly took her sex very seriously. Clint had intended to take her quickly and be done with it, and return downstairs before long.

Rosa had other plans.

For a girl so small, Rosa had more energy than any whore Clint had ever been with. Her body was taut and sleek, and her mouth was educated and eager.

She grabbed for him as he rose from the bed, but he eluded her grasp.

"But we are not finish, Clint," she said.

"Maybe you're not, Rosa," Clint said, "but I am. You're more woman than any one man can handle or satisfy."

"But you satisfy me, Clint," she said, pouting. "Rosa wants you to satisfy her even more."

Under other circumstances Clint would have been glad to stay, but he'd left Sara alone with Bishop and his men long enough.

"Rosa, you take the rest of the night off, you hear?" he said.

"Are you coming back?"

"Maybe," he said. "If I get a chance."

She stretched, and her hard little breasts pointed at the ceiling.

"Then I will wait for you right here."

"You do that."

Clint stepped out into the hall and moved quietly to the top of the stairs. He looked down and saw Sara seated at a table with Bishop next to her, and four other men seated with them. The other two were still sitting together at another table.

When the men had ridden into town, Clint had counted heads. There were nine, plus Pete Bishop. That made ten, and right now seven of them were seated in the *cantina*. If Clint had been Bishop, he'd have a man guarding the gold. That left two men unaccounted for, and if Clint were *them* he'd have headed for the nearest whorehouse.

Clint decided that if he was going to get that gold, tonight was the night, while Sara had most of them occupied looking down the front of her blouse.

Doing it tonight would also keep Sara out of the line of fire.

He turned away from the steps to look for a rear way out. When he didn't find one he considered going back into Rosa's room and using the window, but he decided against it. Instead he tried some of the other doors. He found one open, and the room was empty. He moved to the window, opened it, and stepped out onto the roof. He worked his way down to the edge and then dropped to the ground.

He only hoped that Sara was half as interesting to those men as she appeared to be.

Chapter Thirty-Seven

Sam Forester was content.

He'd just come back from the whorehouse, where a big-breasted whore had done her best to give him a heart attack—and damn near succeeded—and now he was sitting on top of a quarter of a million dollars in gold.

What more could a man want out of life?

Jack Pine went to the whorehouse and asked for the same whore Sam Forester had. Jerry Holden, was *still* upstairs with his whore, one of them wearing the other one out.

Well, Jack Pine was gonna do some wearin' out of his own.

As soon as Jack Pine closed the door and grabbed his whore, Jerry Holden opened the door to the room he'd been in and stepped out into the hall. Jesus, but his legs felt weak. That whore had liked to suck the life out of him.

He decided to go over to the livery to see who was standing guard on the gold. Maybe they'd let him have a look at it before he went to get a bottle.

•   •   •

Sam Forester couldn't help himself. He just had to get
a look at the gold. He knew that Bishop was trusting him
as much as he trusted Pine, but knowing Jack Pine, he
must have peeked.

That was all Sam wanted, a little peek.

What could that hurt?

Clint circled around and came up on the livery stable
from behind. He looked through a window and saw the
light inside. By the glow of a storm lamp he saw a man
on the back of the buckboard, hunched over something.
He was probably supposed to be guarding the gold, but
right now the man looked totally occupied with *looking* at it.

Clint went to the back door, tried it, and found it
locked. He moved around to the side and found a door
there. It was unlocked. It must have been the way the
men who were guarding the gold came and went.

Now it was the way in for Clint.

He opened the door as quietly as he could and slipped
inside. He could hear the buckboard shifting beneath the
man's weight, and he moved toward it.

The man was opening a chest, and Clint moved from
the shadow into the light of the storm lamp. Moving
quickly, he leaped onto the buckboard. The man, feeling
the buckboard shift, turned quickly—but not quickly
enough. Clint brought the barrel of his gun down on the
man's head, sending him sprawling from the buckboard
to the floor of the stable.

Clint hadn't known quite what to expect a quarter of
a million dollars in gold to look like, but there were two
chests on the buckboard. When the man had turned he'd
let the top of the chest he'd been opening drop shut
again. Clint was about to lift the top and have a look

for himself when he heard that side door open.

"Jack! Sam!" a voice called. "Which one of you varmints is in here?"

The man rushed from the darkness into the light of the lamp, and when he saw Clint on top of the buckboard he went for his gun.

Clint had no choice. Either he killed the man, or he'd be killed. Either way, a shot was going to be fired.

He drew his gun very deliberately, while the other man rushed to get his gun out. The other man got off the first shot, but it went wild. Clint fired, catching the man square in the chest. The man dropped his gun and slumped to the floor.

One shot might have gone unnoticed.

But two . . . that was unlikely.

Clint could have regretted his impulse to go after the gold tonight, but he decided he couldn't afford the time.

He had to get out of there.

"What the hell was that?" Pete Bishop snapped, sitting straight up in his chair.

Sara was seated next to him, her chin in her hand, sitting forward so he'd have a clear view of her breasts. She'd found all of this attention very . . . invigorating. Now, however, it was time to get to work.

"What was what?" she asked.

"Did you boys hear it?" Bishop asked.

"It sounded like a shot," one man said.

"Sounded like two shots," another man said.

"Check it out," Bishop said. When only two or three men stood up he added, "All of you."

Grudgingly the other men rose and followed the rest out the door.

"Do you think it's something . . . important?" Sara asked him.

"Shots in Mexico? Have you ever been down here before, Sara?"

"No."

"Then you'd better get used to hearing shots."

What had happened? she wondered. The last she'd seen of Clint he'd been going upstairs with that Mexican whore. She hadn't liked that very much, and had contrived to make him believe that she *hadn't* seen him.

How had he gotten outside, or did he even have anything to do with the shots?

"Sara," Bishop said, putting his hand on hers, "I hope you won't mind if I go out and check things out myself."

Apparently Bishop had just gotten nervous about the gold.

"Oh," she said, pouting, "I thought now that we were alone we could get better acquainted."

"Well," he said, smiling, "I am still on a job, but as soon as I'm finished—"

"What kind of a job?"

His eyes flicked to the front door anxiously.

"I can't say right now," he said, standing up. "I really have to go."

"Without a good-bye kiss?" she said, standing and blocking his way.

"Oh," he said, smiling again.

He stepped forward to take her in his arms, and she put her hands on his waist—and liberated his gun.

She stepped back and pointed the gun at him.

"Don't move, Bishop!"

He frowned, obviously wondering what the hell was going on.

"Don't even think about it," she said. "If you move, I'll use this."

"What's going on?"

"My name is Sara Jones," she said, "and I'm arresting you in the name of Wells Fargo."

"Wells Fargo?"

"That's right," she said. "We want our gold back."

He studied her for a moment, then seemed to relax.

"A lady Wells Fargo agent."

"That's right."

"Well, lady," he said, "I hope you brought a lot of help with you."

Sara was thinking about Clint at that moment. How much help was *she* being to *him* by holding this one man while he had to deal with nine?

Chapter Thirty-Eight

Clint got out of the livery stable just in time. He took refuge in the corral out back and watched as Bishop's men poured into the stable. Two of them stopped just outside.

"Here's our chance," one of them said.

"To do what?"

"To get out of here with the gold."

"How?"

"Whatever happened inside, Bishop's in the *cantina* with the girl, and we're here with the gold. This is our chance, Milt. Let's take the gold and get out of this town."

"We'll have to convince the others."

The first man slapped Milt on the back and said, "They won't take much convincing."

The two men went inside with the rest. Once the door closed behind them, Clint quit the cover of the corral and headed for the *cantina*.

"You're making a big mistake, Sara," Bishop said. "Is that your real name? Sara Jones?"

"It's my real name—and I'd prefer that you call me Miss Jones."

"*Miss* Jones," Bishop said. "Well, does your company know how you dress on duty?"

Bishop inched a little closer, and she backed up and held the gun straight out in front of her, holding it with both hands.

"Don't come any closer!"

Even she noticed that her hands were shaking. Could she shoot this man if he tried to take the gun away from her?

"I'd do what she says," a man's voice said. "She doesn't look too steady to me."

"Clint!" she said, relief flooding through her at the sound of his voice.

"Clint?" Bishop said, eyeing the newcomer.

Clint came into Sara's line of view, and she saw that his gun was still in his holster.

"Clint—" she said.

"Just hold the gun on him, Sara," Clint said. "Right now he's all we've got."

"You mean you didn't get the gold?" she asked. "What was all that shooting?"

"I had the gold," Clint said, "but a second man walked in on me."

"You *had* the gold?"

Clint turned his eyes away from Bishop and looked at Sara for the first time.

"Do you know how much a quarter of a million dollars in gold weighs?"

She hesitated a moment and then said, "No."

"Well . . . neither do I, but it sure as hell weighs too much to fit in my pocket."

"Well, where is it?"

"It's still in the livery, still on the buckboard."

"Clint Adams," Bishop said this time.

"That's right," Clint said.

"Well, what do we do now?" Sara asked.

"We use him to get the gold."

"What the hell brings you to Mexico?" Bishop asked. "I thought you stayed in the United States."

"You thought wrong, Bishop."

"You know who I am?"

"I know you by reputation and description."

"Well, I know you by reputation, too, but I've never heard a description." He frowned at Clint and said, "You were in here before, weren't you?"

"Yeah."

"You and her working together?"

"Sort of," Clint said. "She's working for Wells Fargo, and I'm working for ten percent of the gold."

"You're working for me!" Sara reminded him.

"You're working for her?" Bishop asked with a smile.

"Let's just say we're after the same thing."

"Well, how do you expect to get it?" Bishop asked.

"You're going to get it for us."

"Me?"

"Him?" Sara said.

"How?" Bishop asked.

"Yeah, how?" Sara asked.

"Sara, keep quiet for a while."

"Clint—"

"Be still!"

"How do you intend to use me?" Bishop asked. "You don't think they'll trade all that gold for me, do you?"

"They won't?" Sara asked.

"They won't," Clint said.

"They want me dead," Bishop said, "only they don't have the nerve to do it themselves. They'll let you do it, and then split the gold up themselves."

"Before your boss gets here," Clint said.

Bishop laughed.

"My boss?"

"The brains," Clint said, "the one who planned the robbery."

"Oh," Bishop said, "*that* boss."

"You're all waiting for him to arrive so you can divvy up the gold."

"*I'm* waiting," Bishop said, "trying to keep them from moving on the gold. What you've done now is given them the chance. They won't stop now. We're going to have to work together to keep them from leaving with the gold."

"Work together?" Sara said derisively. "You must be crazy—"

"He's right," Clint said, recalling the conversation he'd just heard outside the livery stable.

"What?"

"I said he's right."

"What do you mean, he's right?" she asked incredulously. "He stole the gold."

"And now that they've got the chance, they'll steal it from him." Clint looked at Sara and said, "I can't stop eight men myself, Sara."

"Nine," Bishop said.

"Eight," Clint said.

"Oh," Bishop said.

"You killed one?" Sara asked.

"Don't start that again," Clint told her.

"No, I didn't mean—"

"Can I have my gun back?"

"Clint—" Sara said, unsure.

"Give it to him, Sara," Clint said. "We're partners now."

"For a while," Pete Bishop said.

"For a while," Clint repeated.

Bishop put his hand out for his gun and, after a

moment of hesitation and an apprehensive glance at Clint, she gave it to him.

"What do we do first . . . partner?" Bishop asked Clint.

Chapter Thirty-Nine

"We don't have time to be fancy," Clint said. "Your men are probably at the livery now, trying to convince each other that now's the time to steal the gold . . . again."

"Do I have time to change?" Sara asked, tugging at the peasant blouse.

"No," Clint said.

"Well, at least let me go back to my room to get my gun."

Clint turned around and looked at the bartender.

"Have you got a shotgun under the bar?"

"*Sí señor.*"

"Give it to me."

The man had no desire to resist Clint. This *gringo* was a dangerous-looking man.

He reached under the bar and came out with an over-and-under shotgun.

"That's fine," Clint said, taking it. He handed it to Sara.

"This really goes with my clothes, doesn't it?"

"Is she really a Wells Fargo agent?" Bishop asked.

"Yep," Clint said, "she really is."

• • •

"Look, Cal," Sam Forester said, "it'll only be another day—"

"What do you think is going to happen when this mysterious Teddy gets here?" Cal Benedict asked.

Forester, bleeding from a gash over his cheekbone, shook his head, which was still fuzzy.

Benedict turned and spoke to the others.

"As soon as he gets here he'll take half—*half!*— for planning the job. Then we split the other half. That is, if Bishop doesn't want half of that. Does that sound fair?"

There was a murmur among the men, expressing disapproval.

"Are we all agreed then?" Cal Benedict asked.

They all began to nod.

"Sam?" Benedict said.

Forester took his hand away from his face and looked at the blood.

"You've shed enough blood for this gold," Benedict said. "Too much to settle for a small part."

"What about Pine?" Forester asked.

"Where is he?" Cal Benedict asked.

"The whorehouse."

"We've got to move now, Sam," Benedict said. He looked at the others and said, "We've got to move now! Right?"

"Right!" they shouted.

"Saddle your horses, then," Benedict said. "Milt, you'll drive the buckboard."

The only thing in all their minds was to take the gold and run. It never occurred to any of them that maybe they could face Bishop together and kill him.

None of them wanted to be the one or two that Pete Bishop's gun would take with him.

•   •   •

"This is a plan?" Sara asked.

They were directly outside the livery.

"Keep your voice down," Clint said. "It's not a plan, exactly. It's a course of action."

"Right," Bishop said.

Sara gave Bishop a sidelong glance that clearly said she still didn't trust him.

"Let me tell you something before we go into this," Bishop said. "I'm a pro, and Adams is a pro. Those fellas in there, they're just . . . trash."

"They're *your* trash," she pointed out.

"My point is *I* was willing to abide by all agreements. *They're* the ones who were planning a double cross."

"And you wouldn't double-cross us?" she asked.

"I wouldn't double-cross *Adams*."

"You don't even know each other!"

"It doesn't matter, Sara," Clint said. "He's right. He and I are pros. We go by our word."

"You trust him?"

"Sure," Clint said, waited a beat, and added, "until after we have the gold."

"That's another story," Bishop said. "I have an obligation to the planner of the job."

"Understood," Clint said. "Just so you know I have obligations as well."

"I understand."

"Are you guys through," she asked, "or is a kiss in order?"

"Just get into position," Clint told her.

"Are we all set?" Benedict asked everyone.

Most of the men were mounted, and the ones who weren't did so now.

"Milt?" Benedict said.

Milt Macklin, seated on the buckboard, picked up the reins and nodded.

"I still think we should have gotten Pine," Sam Forester said.

Benedict ignored him. As far as he was concerned, that was one less share he had to worry about. If he could have he would have taken the gold himself and left, but if Bishop came after them, he'd need help.

Once they were clear, he could think of a way of getting it all for himself.

"Bo," Benedict called out to a man, "you get the doors. Let's get out of this town."

Chapter Forty

It was Clint's opinion that their only chance was to hit them within the constricting confines of the livery, and not to let them get out into the street. To this end he and Bishop would front them when the doors opened, and Sara would slip in the side. That way they'd have them in sort of a cross fire. Before leaving the saloon he'd remembered to get extra shells for the over-and-under from the bartender. It wouldn't have done to leave Sara with just the two shots already loaded in the gun.

Now he and Bishop waited together, and heard the sound of the doors being opened together. They looked at each other and both nodded, drawing their guns.

The doors swung open, and both men started firing.

Sara stood by the side door, waiting for the signal, which would be Clint and Bishop opening fire. When she heard the shots she shoved the door open and leapt inside.

When the twin doors of the livery swung open, Cal Benedict was feeling elated because he'd succeeded in getting the better of Pete Bishop.

As the doors opened Benedict looked outside, and when he saw Bishop and another man standing there, guns drawn, he said, "Oh, shit!" with feeling, and went for his gun.

Bishop's first shot snatched Benedict from his saddle and dumped him on the ground.

Clint took out the man on the ground first, the one who had opened the door, and then shot the man on the buckboard so he couldn't ride them down.

Sara aimed the shotgun and let loose with both barrels, firing into the men gathered into a group in the livery. They had nowhere to go. She heard their screams as double-0 buckshot tore into them, but didn't look. Instead she concentrated on reloading.

Bishop moved closer to the confines of the livery but remained outside. He fired as quickly as he could. Some of the men he hit were already bleeding from buckshot.

Clint was more deliberate. He didn't want to waste a shot on somebody who was already mortally wounded. The lamp in the livery was still lit, and by its garish, yellow glow he picked off men who appeared to have escaped the initial onslaught of the lead storm.

It was over surprisingly quickly. . . .

Jack Pine heard the shots as he was walking to the *cantina,* and broke into a run. When he came into view of the livery he saw what was happening. He recognized immediately that the men in the stable had been outmaneuvered. Trapped inside the livery, they had no chance.

Pine moved closer, waiting for his chance to do a little outmaneuvering of his own.

The moans from inside the livery told Clint and Bishop that all of the men were not dead. They were, however, out of commission.

"Let's check them out," Clint said. "Cover me."

"You're covered."

Clint moved into the livery and began checking bodies. He made sure he kicked the guns away from those who were still breathing.

Sara came from the back, holding her shotgun ready. From the glazed look in her eyes Clint knew she was on the verge of hysteria.

"It's over, Sara," he said, moving close to her.

She looked at him, but he didn't think she really saw him.

"You did fine," he said, taking the shotgun from her. She didn't resist. "You did just fine."

That was when they heard the shot.

Jack Pine watched the other man go into the livery and knew that this was his chance. Bishop had turned on them, and he deserved whatever he got.

He took out his gun, pointed, and shot Pete Bishop in the back.

Clint ran outside in time to see Bishop fall. His eyes swept the dark street, illuminated only by moonlight, and saw the man pointing the gun at him now. He dropped to the ground and fired, but in his haste his shot missed.

Dropping to the ground, however, had caused the other man to miss as well. The assailant didn't wait to fire again. He started running down the street.

"Take care of Bishop!" Clint shouted, getting to his feet and taking after the man.

Clint could have let the man go. After all, they had the gold, and all of the other men were dead, dying, or badly wounded. What did one more man matter?

Except that this man had committed what was considered the cardinal sin by men in Clint's profession.

He had shot another man in the back.

The act of a gutless, spineless coward.

Clint chased the man down the main street, never losing sight of him. Even from where he was he could hear the man's labored, panicky breathing and he knew he had him.

The man turned down an alley next to the *cantina*, and Clint moved to the mouth of the alley and flattened himself against the building.

He knew from his initial turn around the town the first day he arrived that the alley had a dead end.

"Nowhere to go, friend!" he shouted. "Toss your gun out and come out after it!"

There was a long period during which Clint could hear the man's raspy breathing, and then a gun came flying out.

"I'm comin out!" the man shouted. "I ain't armed!"

"Come ahead."

Clint stepped away from the building and waited for the man to appear, arms in the air.

"I'm givin' up," the man said nervously. "I ain't armed."

"Open your mouth," Clint said.

"What?"

Clint moved closer and jammed his gun into the man's throat.

"Open your mouth."

"What for?"

"Open it!" he said, jamming the barrel of the gun against the man's throat so hard that he choked.

He opened his mouth, and Clint placed the barrel of the gun inside. The metal was still hot, and the man flinched.

"You shot a man in the back, friend," Clint said. "That earns you a one-way ticket to hell."

The man's eyes widened as he realized what Clint was going to do, and then Clint pulled the trigger.

Chapter Forty-One

Pete Bishop died.

So did six of the men in the livery that night. The others would soon, since there was no doctor in town.

Sara, after finding out what Clint had done to the man who'd shot Bishop, never looked at him in the same way. Any attraction she had felt for him was gone. She could never feel anything for a man who was so . . . ruthless.

She would have liked to leave the next day with the gold, but Clint told her they had to wait.

"What for?"

"For the brains to come riding in."

"How will we know him?"

"We'll know him," Clint said. "After we take him, you can have the gold."

"And you your ten percent."

"And then we'll go our separate ways."

"Yes," she said with a touch of sadness.

Two days after the shootout at the livery stable, Officer Pressman of the Caliente Police Department came riding into town.

Clint wasn't one bit surprised.

ANGEL EYES *series*
by
Award-Winning Author
Robert J. Randisi (J.R. Roberts)

Visit us at www.speakingvolumes.us

TRACKER *series*
by
Award-Winning Author
Robert J. Randisi (J.R. Roberts)

Visit us at <u>www.speakingvolumes.us</u>

MOUNTAIN JACK PIKE *series*
by
Award-Winning Author
Robert J. Randisi (J.R. Roberts)

Visit us at www.speakingvolumes.us